FREDDY SCURRY

STUCK

A GANGSTA'S MATRIX

A Genuine Life Ent. Presentation

GENUINE LIFE ENTERTAINMENT

P.O.BOX 9182

Augusta, GA 33916

ACKNOWLEDGMENTS

First giving honor to GOD, to whom I seek first, for approval. Without him, I am nothing!!

To my momma, he keep throwing us blessings, we just have to continue to receive them as such. You've been praying for me before I ever knew what prayer meant. Forever loving you! Big Daddy, it wasn't always cool, but you were there, preciate ya!! Without the struggle, we probably would've never OVERSTOOD the mission.

Nikki, Nikki, Nikki! Everybody already know what it is with us. Everyday ain't gonna always be great, so I'm blessed to know I got somebody who gonna be there despite! It's true that we ain't in love every second of the day, but I haven't met the perfect family yet either. Besides we have Tre and Da'mon to think about, so it really ain't about us all the time either. Dam, can't win for losing, huh?!!!!

To the fam; Ron, Tamika, Lil John and Elisha. It's been a ride, but we still all alive and healthy. Our positions out here is solely up to us. Success is

4

only a block away. Na'll, I ain't forgot about Janae, Lil James, Tameka and Jamedira. I love ya'll too and our time is definitely coming. Thanks to James Moore Sr., we long over do.

To all my brethren, as you read this you already know who you are. Thank ya'll, for the smiles and frowns. It takes a special type of person to stay focus throughout them both. It's been a blessing to come across some of you cats, while others, it's been a blessing we kept a distance. Like I said, you know who you are!

To everybody that knows they had something to do with this and any other venture I've been involved in, I preciate ya! I'll be writing for days giving names, and the book already long enough.

Shout out to the MIAMI HEAT, ATLANTA FALCONS, "THE U" and DUKE. That's who I ride with, most already know!!! Let's get it!!!!

I almost forgot, to every GENUINE individual, and I say GENUINE because, being real just ain't enough no more!! My bad, there I go again. To every GENUINE individual out there, please continue to stand up and live that GENUINE LIFE! PRECIATE YA'LL!!!!!!!!!!!!

STUCK

Every way of man is right in his own eyes: but the LORD pondereth the heart.

Pro. 21:2

PROLOGUE

For the last few years, this life I've been living has been a constant trial after trial. It seems as if every time I get past one obstacle, I'm right back in the mist of another. I guess you could say that I was just another youngster on a mission striving to find his place in this cruel world.

During the mist of my quest I was introduced to so much negativity, that eventually, I was pushed in the vicious hands of Babylon's modern day servants. Within hours I went from hearing the constant irritable sounds of gun shots and sirens to hearing these steel doors open and close every hour or so. But on this cold day in February, all that has had my full attention will be completely out of my sight.

"Mr. Pearsey, are you ready?" Is what I heard the female officer ask as she walked inside my two-man cell.

"Wouldn't you be, Ms. Davis?" I sarcastically responded as I grabbed my manila folder from the steel desk.

"Deamon, is that really all you're leaving with?" She inquired with a seductive look of delight.

I really was digging this woman, so when I looked into her enticing green eyes, I couldn't help but smile before replying, "You know, I might can get use to you saying my name like that."

"Well, I guess that's just something you gotta do," she implied as she handed me a piece of paper with her number on it.

Officer Teresa Davis just happened to be the sexiest female on the yard. She stood around five-seven with about one hundred and twenty-five pounds accommodating her pecan-tan complexion. Even though her hair hung a little past her shoulders, she kept it pinned up like a true stallion. Oh yeah, did I happen to mention those mesmerizing green eyes?!

From where I was standing, it seemed that every cat on the yard longed for just a few moments with her. Hell, from time to time, I even witnessed the gay cats stare at her with that lustful look of hunger.

"You know you picked a fine time to give me this number," I voiced with a disapproving expression as I held the paper up to her face.

"Better late than never," is what she had the nerve to say while lightly pushing my hand away, "but if you play your cards right you'll see that it was well worth the wait."

She was now so close to me that I could feel her breathing on my neck. Her presence had already taken me to higher heights, but to add on to that, out of nowhere I felt her tongue lashing across my ear. From her minor seducing, along with the excitement of me being released, I was only seconds away from losing my composure.

"Is this what every cat gets when he leaves here?" I managed to ask with a smirk.

"Don't try to play me, Deamon!" She retorted with that same phony cold stare that I've come accustomed to seeing these past seven months.

See, we've been conversing on the regular. I admit, it took a while for her to let her guard down long enough to even speak on the matters of a relationship. But with me being so persistent, it wasn't long before I had her stopping by my cell with little notes that told me what type of panties she was wearing. Hell, just a few months ago I almost had her....

She was running gym call that morning and since I was forced to attend, either that or sit in my cell and wait for the warden to come through for inspection. Besides, a few cats had already been taunting me about hooping.

It was a surprise to us all to see her in the gym. A few cats practically ran over to greet her, while the rest of us walked to the back to dress out. After sliding my shorts on, I grabbed a ball and acted as if she wasn't even there.

It was already all over the yard that we was kicking it, so I really wasn't interested in adding heat to that flame. To her, it obviously didn't matter, one way or the other, because every time I looked in her direction our eyes met. It was as if she wanted everyone to know that it was I who had her full attention.

"Good morning Mr. Pearsey," is how she greeted me after her fan club parted, "you know I can't recall waking up next to you."

"You sound as if you wasn't too happy about that," is all I managed to reply with.

"Well, I see that I've found that ole slick mouth person to clean up when gym's over," she declared with a seductive smile.

"You know that I never had a problem with

that," I replied with a smile of my own.

It was one lost and three wins later when she finally called gym over.

"Pearsey, I hope that you don't think that you're gonna sneak out of here!" She yells from the other side of the gym before adding, "You know that you're my orderly, for the time being!"

I hated the fact that I was gonna be around her all sweaty, but I had already committed, so I definitely couldn't back out now. So as she patted everyone down, I grabbed the dust- mop and pushed it over the gym floor.

"Don't forget to hit the office windows, the warden is supposed to be coming through to inspect," is what she finally mentioned as the last cat walked out the gym.

"I could've stayed in the dorm if I wanted to see the warden!" I stressed with probably too much aggression.

After recognizing that I was a little uncomfortable, she walks over to me with that sarcastic expression and questions, "Now I know Mr. Pearsey ain't scared of the warden?"

"Now see, that's where you have things twisted, cause it ain't even about being scared, it's about staying out of these folk's face."

"Baby, he's just gonna walk in and walk out. I promise that I'm not gonna let him come in here and bother you boo," she assure me along with a wink of her eye before walking in the office.

It wasn't but ten minutes later that him and his goons came through and did just what she said he would. The moment he walked out, I walked towards the back to get dress.

"Now was that so bad?" Is what she asked as she trailed me.

"I guess not."

"You know that you owe me an apology," she practically demanded, openly catching me off guard.

"For what?" I challenged as I looked down into those tantalizing eyes of hers.

"For not acknowledging me when you saw me," she humbly replied with a look of disappointment as she stroked my face with her hand, "you obviously don't know that everytime you come to mind, she gets to thinking on her own."

Now, I must admit that I wasn't really prepared for what she had just said, but I definitely wasn't prepared for what happened next. She smoothly grabbed my hand and placed it where I could feel just what she was talking about.

Say what you feel, but baby-girl was beyond moist. She was erupting like a volcano as she let loose her hot lava all over my blessed fingers. As my fingers marinated in the mist of her foils, her eyes closed.

She wrestled with my shorts for what she seemed to be longing for. After finally grasping it, she looked up at me with a satisfied expression as she bit her bottom lip. I rotated her clit in a slow and easy stride as she stroked me. Now, if I wasn't so concentrated on pleasing her, I know I would've erupted the moment she touched me.

A loud moan and the stiffness of her body assured me that she had indeed climaxed. Through it all, despite her own condition, she never stop trying to make sure that I joined her in ecstasy. Just when I erupted, someone knocked on the door, bringing us both back to the gym in this state penitentiary.

I rushed my clothes on and headed for the door, while she scurried towards the office. Just my luck, it was the same sergeant who'd been trying to throw me in the hole for whatever, while at the same time trying to get at Officer Davis.

"Pearsey, they waiting for you back in the dorm, its count time," is what he stressed with a disturbing expression.

Now, I really don't know why he was trying to play me for slow, cause the expression on his face told me that I was the last person he was expecting to see in here.

"My bad sarge, I guess I couldn't hear over the buffer," is how I replied after seeing a buffer still plugged up from the previous night.

He nodded his head after noticing the buffer in the corner. I paid the hater no mind as I walked to the office to let her know that I was headed back to the dorm. She nodded her head with a smile and I moved out of the hater's way...

We were now headed down the walk toward classification to get my paperwork out of this concrete jungle.

Right before we stepped in the building, she reached in her pocket and pulled out two hundred dollar bills and handed them to me. When I looked up at her, she seemed as if she was more thrilled than me.

"I know that it ain't much, but I wanted you to leave with some cash in your pocket," she practically proclaimed with a huge grin on her face.

"You know you stay surprising a playa," I stressed with a smile of my own before I kissed her on the cheek.

"Baby-boy, you just wait until you make that phone call," is what I heard her say before I walked through the classification door...

"State your name, height, weight, age and state number please?" The I.D. Officer asked for verification of who I was.

"Deamon Pearsey, six-one, one-hundred ninety-five pounds, twenty years old and my number is 329199."

"You know that you have a long life ahead of you Mr. Pearsey, you just have to find a way to stay out of places like this," she preached as if she wasn't really concerned, but as if it was a part of her job.

I remained silent until we were walking out the back door, "You know leaving here will be the best thing that ever happened to me."

"It also can turn out to be the worst!" She

retorted with a blank expression as we walked
through the final gate of this unjust correctional
facility.

(CHAPTER 1)

-TERESA-

It's been eight months since I last saw him. He was all I ever wanted in a man. At the time, it seemed as if he was the only one who understood me. Yeah he was thuggish, yet, at the same time, sensitive. It never mattered to me that he sold drugs, because I never was introduced to that side of him.

When he was with me, all we ever talked about was our future together. The Lord knows that I really loved that man, but now, after all he's taken me through, I hate him and everything he stands for.

I hate him for not paying attention to his surroundings and not knowing that federal agents were watching his every move. I hate him for trusting Eddie Butler enough to ride around and talk about deals while he wore a wire for the Feds.

I told him that I never really cared for Eddie, but no, he and Eddie grew up together. They jumped in the game together, so I guess he is more than happy that they are doing their federal time together!

18

There my slow ass was, twenty-two years old planning a life with someone who puts their freedom in jeopardy every day. I can still remember how it all went down as if it was yesterday when his ass called me at work....

"Baby-girl, I'm not gonna be home for a while," is what I remembered him saying..

"And why is that David?" My dumb ass had the nerve to ask.

"The Feds just busted me and Eddie at his house."

I didn't know what to do, so I just hung the phone up and headed straight for Eddie's house. That day I lost out big time. I lost my job at the dentist office, my car and what I thought then, the love of my life.

"Ms. Davis, don't try to move," the nurse standing over me was saying, "you're in Memorial Hospital. You were in a car accident, but you're gonna be alright. You might feel a little pain because you suffered a minor concussion and you have two broken ribs."

"But, what about David?" I managed to ask right before I remembered why I was in such a rush to get to Eddie's house.

STUCK

I never understood what Toya saw in Eddie's ass anyway. Besides, the little money he was getting, he was nothing.

I felt so awful as I laid there and watched the same bitch I caught David fucking a few months prior, read his charges out on the channel twelve news with no remorse.

"David Battle and Eddie Butler has been charged with trafficking cocaine. Federal agents, along with the local authorities seized seven and a half pounds of the illegal substance during a raid at 1907 Paradise Park on the south side of Savannah. Authorities say that they've been investigating Mr. Battle and Mr. Butler for quite some time."

Lord knows that I cried for weeks after, but hey, that was eight months ago. I've now started a new life. I have a new job and hopefully I've found the right man. I know that he's a little younger than me, but at least he seems to know what he wants out of life. And it really doesn't hurt that he's tall, dark and as fine as they come these days.

So what, he's been locked up! I don't know about anybody else, but I'd rather get them coming out, then right before they're going in.

Yeah I know that he just got out Thursday, but here it is Tuesday and I still haven't heard from him. What really irks me is the fact that I never realized that my feelings for him was this strong.

I really went through a lot with the David situation, and I guess you can say that he helped me get through that. I never meant for things to go as far as they have with us, but he actually made me feel whole again.

When I first started working at the prison, I had no interest in talking to anyone, especially an inmate. But, one day they had me working in medical where I had to at the least, ask what they needed. I didn't even noticed when he walked in, and to be honest, at that time I didn't care to see.

"You don't have to look like that," he said, "life can't be that bad, you free ain't you?"

"Excuse me inmate?" I questioned in a harsh manner.

"You know we all go through obstacles that seem unbearable at times, but you strong enough. Besides, most of us can see through all that phony hard shit."

As bad as I wanted to say something hateful, nothing seemed to escape my lips. It's like he picked me. I mean, he knew exactly what to say

21

and that literally had me spellbound. As I watched him walk out that door, I knew I had to find out who he was.

At first I was really pissed at myself for revealing my emotional stress so vividly. I hated the fact that he'd picked me so easily, but my eagerness to find out who he was out weighed all of that.

For the last eight months I'd dealt with my issues on my own. It was really times that I was ready to give up, but what this dude had just said to me really gave me a little inspiration.

Deamon Pearsey was his name and he definitely had me open. Now, I just had to find out who he was, without exposing my motives.

I was still sitting behind the desk contemplating how I was gonna do just that, when the nurse brought to my attention that he had left his identification in her station. Now as I was considering hand delivering his I.D., this mysterious dude walks right back through the door.

"Excuse me, Ms. Davis, but I think that I left my I.D. in the nurse's station."

"Well, you know that you're gonna have to clean this area to get this card back."

"But, it's about to be count time. Besides, don't you have orderlies for that?" He rebutted.

"Well, all of my orderlies have gone in for count and it really isn't nothing for me to put you on my count list," I recovered, using my authority to the max.

"In the future just let me know when you want me to keep you company," he replied with a smile, revealing the fact that he had gold fronts.

"The broom and mop are in the closet, second door on the right," I stated with a light smile of my own.

I swear this dude asked me one question, "So what's going on in that pretty little head of yours?" And I practically told him everything.

I didn't realize how much I had ran my mouth, until I heard that count was clear over my radio. Now I have to admit that I really felt good about getting it all out, but I also felt kind of funny about me spilling my guts to an inmate, especially one that I knew nothing about.

He must have read my mind because he said, "You know we all need someone to talk to at times, and we never really know who that person might be. It's like we can't talk to people because we don't trust them, or maybe we just feel that nobody can really feel where we be coming from or what we're going through. But I have to let you know, that talking to you today has made me feel 100% better than I was feeling before I walked in here. So maybe one day we can finish this conversation."

"Maybe we can," was the only reply I could conjure up.

Since that day we have bonded like no other. He's helped me grasp strength that I didn't even know I had possession of.

But now his ass has me sitting by this phone waiting on him to call, to at the least, say hello. I mean, doesn't he know that I need him? Doesn't he know that I want him? I mean doesn't he know that I love him?!

Hell no! I know I just didn't say that! But hell, I do, and his ass knows, doesn't he?

I know one thing, I'm not about to sit here like a fool and just wait on him to call. If he doesn't call me tonight, I will be taking my ass to Augusta tomorrow.

-KRUGER-

With Makevelli's, 'White Man's World', playing through the speakers that my brother has mounted in every corner of the room, and a half a fifth of *Hennessy*, the mood was just right. My only problem is this leg monitor these folks surprised me with when I stepped out.

I've been trapped in this house for a week, so I haven't had the chance to do too much of anything. But tomorrow, I'm supposed to be able to go out to look for a job, hopefully these folks don't renege on that.

Luckily, I had some money on my books when I got out, because it's hell out here for a hustler. When a warrior gets out of prison, you would expect a little more than a hug, but in another since it's all good. You really don't want to get out, looking for a handout. Because, usually, the first person who looks out for you, you're kind of obligated to have some sense of loyalty to them. At least that's how we was taught. That's why a playa has to be careful where he look for help at.

Take Teresa for example. She hit a playa with the two bills, so I know she probably hot right now, because I haven't hit her up yet. Physically, she's a star, but on a mental and emotional aspect she has issues.

Now, I ain't saying that everything is all roses on my end, but it's really no secret in regards to what I'm about to get my hands into. With that in mind, it really ain't wise to take that relationship outside those walls and gates. Without a doubt, me and her was cool, but I was also able to see firsthand her true level of loyalty through the way she treats that cat David.

Now maybe it's just me, but I feel regardless of the trial, if you know that someone has had your back, in any way, we're obligated to show that same level of consideration. I mean she would always mentioned the fact that he always made sure she was straight on the financial tip. Hell, at least strive to give him that back.

It's bad enough that she doesn't accept his phone calls or write, but at least show some love to him on his books. To me, loyalty is a serious virtue that more than often gets neglected. I guess you can say that I feel so strongly on the issue because of Surina.

Surina was as close to a mate as I ever had. What David is going through with Teresa, I caught the same heat from Surina.

Surina is this red bone with an apple bottom, Luke dancer's body. To top it all off she possessed a face as cute as Grant Hill's wife. She's what we call, a true ghetto trophy. And I guess the thing is, I'm afraid that Teresa is no different.

It's like they're your lady as long you can dish out whatever, when they want it, but when you're trapped and money gone, you're dead wrong! On one hand they're in the right, because we are supposed to be out here preparing for all obstacles, so on that aspect, we slipping.

Now since I've been home, Surina has been calling the house on the hunt for me, but I'll just have somebody tell her that I'm not here. I mean, really, look at this here. I just did two years behind them walls and fences, and she just now trying to go out her way to get at me. Now picture me being that slow.

It's like I heard the rapper 8-Ball say, "Your status seems to be built on the baddest shit you can afford!" And that seems to be the case with these females. So yeah, I can feel what ole boy David is going through.

"Boy, if you don't turn that noise down!" is what I hear my mama yell as she bams on the door.

27

"Yes, mamm," I responded as I slid the cognac bottle under my pillow.

"Open this door!" She stated as if I was still ten years old.

"It's open."

After walking in and surveying the room, she said, "Me and your sister about to go to bible study. I wish you didn't have that thing on your leg, because I'll make your butt go to."

"I know mama."

"Deamon!" My sister yells from the kitchen.

"What, girl?!" I yelled backed before getting an ugly look from my mama for yelling in her ear.

"Some girl name Teresa just called and said that she on her way over here."

"What you mean, she on her way over here?!" I responded with a confused expression.

"Just what I said!" She retorted, "She called here like ten minutes ago and said that she was on Tobacco Road, so I gave her directions."

"Now, what part of the game is this?" Is what I found myself whispering out as I looked over at my mama.

After she saw the expression on my face

28

she giggled and finally said, "Girl, you didn't know if he wanted company."

"He wanna see her mama, she coming all the way from Savannah," my sister revealed as she walked into the room with a devious smirk.

Now a lot of people say that we look alike, but right now I just can't see it. All I can see at the moment is a future drama queen.

"Mama, I don't wanna go to bible study," she stressed, "I wanna stay here so I can see Surina swing on Deamon when she catches that other girl over here."

"Say what?!" I can't believe this here, "How she know I'm here?"

"Girl, go and get your coat so we can go, and leave that boy alone," my mama finally spoke up and stressed.

"Is that all you gonna say to her?" I questioned.

"Listen boy, if you don't wanna mess with that girl Surina, tonight will be a good time to let her know. I'm tired of her calling here all day anyway," she indicated as she walked away.

Now my mama has to be the strongest woman I know. She's a devoted wife of a Baptist preacher, the mother of five and a educator. I've witnessed her overcome a lot. Whether she knows it or not she's my greatest inspiration. So whenever she spoke, I listened.

As far as me and her husband was concerned, we stayed with animosity in the air. He was the main reason I stayed in my room with the door closed. With him being a preacher and me being in the streets, we was never able to see eye to eye. He was just as ready for this monitor to come off my leg as I was.

I guess its mad beef because I feel he spends too much time trying to aid a church, who is clearly more enthused by the way he dresses than the message he strives to bring forth on Sunday, than he was of his own family.

It's like he can't see that Tamika don't dig church too funny, or that Lil Benny was failing in school. Sometimes it was hard to see that he was aware that my baby brother Lil Man was making straight A's. If you ask me, I just feel that he should sweep around his own front door before he goes to clean up somebody else's. But hell, what do I know, I'm the sinner!

"Bye Deamon," Tamika stressed with a sly grin as she walked towards the front door.

"It's all good, because sooner or later you're gonna need something."

"I know, and you'll be the first one to give it to me," is how she responded as she walked out of the house.

Now when I think about it, she might've did me a favor. I can really use this to my advantage if I play it like it supposed to be played. I mean I really don't wanna mess with either one of them, not like that anyway. So it might be good for them both to meet up. That way they both will know where we stand.

-TERESA-

"Girl, just wait until you see him," I was saying to Toya.

"Calm down!" She snapped back, "And don't let this dude get you like that, hell, he's too young anyway!"

Now Toya has been my best friend since the eighth grade. That was when she stop the school butch, Bridgette, from making a fool out of me. So now she really thinks she runs my life.

"Girl, this young cat better be all that you say he is the way that you keep carrying on!" Is what she pointed out as she drove her Mazda 626 that her snitching ass boyfriend bought her, "Teresa, I know I told you to move on, but I didn't mean all the way here in Augusta!"

I can't really blame her for being frustrated, because it's been twenty minutes since I talked to his sister who said that we were only ten minutes away.

"There it go right there girl! Turn right, turn right—right here!" I practically screamed.

"Dam girl!" She yelled back, "I see the sign!"

"I'm sorry, I just didn't want you to miss the turn."

She always makes me feel as if I'm in the wrong. I know her ass would really trip if she knew that we're just popping up over here. I should have at least called and let him know that I was coming, but it ain't no need to trip now, we here.

"Teresa, are you alright?" She asked in a concerned manner.

"Yeah girl, just nervous as hell," I replied while looking out the passenger window.

"Well, here is Leawood Court," she

32

announced as if she was trying to knock me out of my trance.

"Their house should be the last one in the corner."

"Call him and tell him to come outside!" Is what she practically insisted in an impatient manner.

I knew that she was tired of me bickering about him, so I just brushed her attitude off and called. I just hope that he don't start tripping, even though he has every right to.

"Hello," a deep voice answered after the second ring.

"May I speak with Deamon?"

"Who this?" He asked.

"Teresa."

"Hold on," he replied right before he called out my boo's name.

Seconds later he was on the phone, "What's up Ms. Sexy?"

"Hey baby, what you doing?" Is all I managed to reply with.

"Chillen, but what's really good with you?"

"Nothing really, I'm just sitting outside

waiting for you," I answered in one of my sexiest voices.

"Yeah, I heard that you was only a few minutes away," he plainly replied before adding, "I'll be out there in a second, just let me put some clothes on."

"You know that I wouldn't mind if you kept them off."

"You know I like it when you talk like that, but I'm on my way out."

"Alright," is all I could get out before the line went dead.

That nigga know that he sounds sexy as hell on the phone.

"So what did he say?" Toya asked.

I had done forgot that she was even here, just that quick.

"He'll be out in a minute," I responded as I put my phone in my purse.

"Well he needs to hurry up, because it's cold out here," she stressed as she pulled up in the driveway.

"Don't rush him," I replied with a huge grin on my face.

"Do he know that he has you like that?" She demanded to know after seeing the way I was glowing.

"He ain't got me like nothing!" I retorted.

"Whatever," she spat out with a sly smirk.

I knew that she was happy that I finally found someone to blush about after David. After everything went down with him and Eddie, she confessed that she knew Eddie was working with the Feds. Of course I was mad for a while, but me and her has been cool a long time before we knew who David or Eddie was.

"You know, I think that was his older brother who answered the phone," I implied, knowing that her thirsty ass would bite the bait.

"How he look?"

"From the picture that I saw of him, he's straight."

"Girl, is that Deamon at the door?" She asked as she pointed towards the house.

He was standing on the porch with a huge smile. Even as we sat in the car we could see the waves in his head as he stood under the porch light. He wore a brown windbreaker with the matching shorts so I could see his bow-legs.

35

As he walked over to the car he looked as if he was happy to see me. Well, at least that's what I hope he was thinking.

"Are ya'll gonna stay in the car all night?" He asked after opening the door for me.

Dam he was fine! And from the look on Toya's face, she was thinking the same thing. I took a quick glance of my boo from head to toe, and that's when I noticed the brace on his leg.

"So what's up with the brace?" I asked with a disapproving expression.

"Just something the parole board surprised me with when I stepped out," he replied as he helped me out the car.

"So how long you have to be on that?"

"Three months."

He wasn't giving me any real feedback, so I was sort of relieved when Toya stepped in and said, "Hey Deamon, I'm Toya, since everybody else seems to have lost their manners."

She then had the nerve to roll her eyes at me before stressing, "Please tell me that you have a twin brother!"

"Toya," I sort of whined out, because I couldn't believe that she had actually asked him that.

He just blushed before replying with, "Na'll, but I do have a brother you might be interested in."

When we walked in the house, we both were impressed with how his parents had decorated. From the ceiling to the floor the house was like whoa!

Now I'm not familiar with all the different types of furniture, but Toya was walking through and appraising everything. I guess with her being the manager at a furniture store, she sort of has the eye for it.

We was sitting on the cream colored couch when his brother walked in the room.

He was tall, husky and a little lighter than Deamon, who always claimed to be the black sheep of the family. I looked over at Toya and could tell that she was impressed with this cat.

"What up playboy?" Deamon greeted him.

"Who is these people, bra?" He replied while smiling over at Toya, who was now blushing.

"Ron, this is Teresa, the police woman I told you about, and that's her friend Toya," is the way he had the nerve to introduce us.

I slapped his leg and stressed, "I ain't no

police woman!"

That caused everyone to burst out laughing. I was relieved, given that we needed to break the ice, seeing as it was kind of getting uncomfortable sitting there, especially with Toya, knowing that she'll say pretty much anything.

"Where you about to go?" Deamon asked his brother as he saw him grabbed his coat.

"No where really, I was just gonna dip and grab a bottle."

"You know that I have a little something in the back," Deamon assured.

"Not no more you don't," Ron replied with a wide grin.

"Man, if you done drunk all that, you know you can't be driving," Deamon stated in a concerned manner.

"So, who's driving?" His brother asked as he focused on Toya.

"Me," she replied in a bashful manner.

"So, are you gonna take me to get something to drink, or what?"

"Man, I've been driving for over three hours trying to find this house, so you gotta drive!"

She answered back as she raised from the couch.

When they reached the door I heard her ask him, "Can you drive stick?"

He just laughed before replying with, "I can drive a stick shift, but hopefully you can drive stick."

"It all depends on how big the stick is," her freaky ass stated.

"Big enough," is what I heard him say as he closed the door behind them.

Deamon raised from next to me and walked towards the door and I was right behind him. After he locked the door and turned around, I lightly pushed him to the wall.

"I missed you," is what I practically whispered.

This was our first real moment alone with no outer disturbance. We just stood there for a moment and gazed into each other eyes before he finally decided to lean over and passionately kiss me. At that moment I felt as if I was where I belonged.

In his arms I felt safe, secure and sexually aroused at the same dam time. Or maybe I was so sexually aroused because I felt so safe and secure.

STUCK

This was definitely a rare moment that I was wishing never ended, and from his reaction, the feeling was mutual.

I eased my mouth from his, to his chin. From his chin to his neck, as I grasped the hardening in his shorts. At that moment I felt more than obligated to release it from its temporary bondage.

After he smoothly took his jacket off, I couldn't help but kiss all over his chiseled chest. I held on to his dick with a grip so tight that you would think that this was the last time I would ever hold one. As I made my way on my knees, I couldn't help but smile, after seeing that lustful look in his eyes.

"I got you baby?" Is what I whispered before inserting him in my mouth.

I took as much of him as I could, causing his body to jerk before he let out a loud moan. I moved in a slow and passionate stride that had him whimpering, so I knew that his time was near.

Out of nowhere he grabbed my arms and picked me up as if I only weighed twenty pounds. I wrapped my legs around his waist and my arms around his neck as he carried me down the hall to the far room on the right.

"Hit that light switch," he stated after stopping at the door.

After I cut the light on he laid me on top of a burgundy and beige paisley comforter that draped the queen sized bed. He then grabbed the remote that was right next to me and pressed a few buttons. A few seconds later the sounds of LSG's, 'My Body', flowed through the speakers.

He started to undress me. First my shoes and socks. Then it seems as if everything else just fell off. Before I knew it I was completely naked with him kissing all over me. He'd made it down to my waist before I stopped him and flipped the whole scene.

"Na'll boo, today is your day," I uttered out as I pushed him up.

I pulled his shorts and boxers off as quickly as I could. I immediately crawled over him and started back where I left off when we was at the front door. Just as soon as I felt that he couldn't get any harder, I straddled him.

Lord knows that I needed this!

After he was completely inside me, I just sat there and gazed down into his eyes for a moment before stating, "You know I should be punishing you for not calling me."

41

"Well, at least give me the opportunity to explain myself," he managed to utter out.

"Save it," I responded before I started maneuvering as if I was on a horse.

After a good two minutes he exploded inside of me. I was so disappointed, until almost instantly he was right back hard as a brick. Feeling him change up inside of me turned me on more than anything, so I went right back to grinding.

Moments later I found myself going through the same process he'd just experienced. I was so zoned out that I couldn't hear anything and all I could see was his face.

"You alright baby-girl?" Is what I finally heard him ask.

"Yeah boo, I guess," I replied right before I heard the doorbell rang, "you wanna get that?"

"And miss all of this!" He stressed as his hands explored my body.

I started to get off of him, but he stopped me and asked, "Where do you think you're going?"

He then placed me in my favorite position. Right before he entered me from the back, he ran his tongue up my spine. That alone caused me to freeze up. This dude really had me going for a minute, but it wasn't long before I was matching his strokes, stride for stride, as we both looked to put the finishing touches on this moment, without missing a beat.

He grabbed and pulled on my hair with his right hand, while he grabbed and squeezed my breast with his left. The moment I looked back at him, it's like it happened, we both erupted. I collapsed and laid on my stomach and he collapsed next to me.

"Dam baby-girl, what is it you trying to do to me?" He asked in a hoarse voice.

"All I wanna do is keep you happy and make you mine," I confessed.

"Well, you're starting off on the right track," he assured me as he looked into my eyes.

"Well, I do what I can when I can, but we both know that was well over do," I replied right before I heard a car horn.

"That's Ron and your girl right there," he stressed.

"How you know?"

"Because that's my brother, and I know my brother," he replied as he raised up before adding, "the bathroom is down the hall, make sure you

43

meet me there in a minute."

The bathroom was as nice as the rest of the house. I was searching for the wash rags when he stepped in with two and matching towels.

"You haven't taken those clothes off yet?" He grilled as he practically slid out of his.

"I can't take a shower with you in your parent's house!" I attempted to protest.

"Girl, if you don't take that shit off!"

(CHAPTER 2)

Jimmy Klein sat in his black Q-45, while on the phone with his girl.

"Where you at?" She asked him.

"I'm sitting in front of A-1 Flea-Market waiting on Weasel to come out," he replied.

Weasel was Jimmy's right hand man. Whenever any enforcing was needed, Jimmy relied on Weasel.

"Say baby-girl, here Weasel come now, so I'll get back at you just as soon as I take care of a few things," he declared as he saw Weasel walking towards the car.

"Alright boo," she responded without a fight, and that really irked him.

Weasel could tell that something more than their current situation was on his mind, the second he sat in the car.

"What's up with you?" Weasel asked as he grabbed the half a blunt from the ash-tray.

"Did you get the scale?" Jimmy responded

45

while pulling out of the parking lot.

"Na'll, they out over here," he replied before firing the blunt up and adding, "but they called 4-Corners, by the car wash, and they say they got two left."

"We might as well get both of them, so we won't have to go through this shit no more."

He had lost a little over 250 grams, a scale and a pistol the night before. Someone broke into the trunk of the Regal he had parked in his mother's backyard.

The loss wasn't the real concern being that it only represented 35% of his profit. Besides, it only took one phone call and thirty minutes for him to get a fresh package.

"Say Weasel," he said as he pulled in the parking-lot of 4-Corners.

"Yeah playboy, what up?" Weasel replied as he turned down the sounds of 8-Ball and MJG.

"You know that it's gonna be hard to pin-point who hit us last night."

Now that was one thing Weasel loved and respected about Jimmy. It was never just his with him, it was always theirs.

"I can feel you, being that a million

muthafuckas know where your mama stay," he agreed while passing him the blunt.

"You know that little lick was really nothing, but we still have to find out who hit us, so we can set an example out here."

"And you already know that I'm on top of it!" Weasel assured before he stepped out of the car.

Despite their loss, Jimmy had other things on his mind. He was wondering what was really going on with his girl, because she'd really been acting out of character lately. She would usually argue him down about how much time he spent in the streets, but she'd been too cool with it lately, so he knew that something was going on.

✱✱✱✱✱✱✱✱✱✱✱✱✱✱

"Deamon, you need to hurry up, because it's a must you get this phone today!" Teresa was stressing while tying her sneakers.

Toya and Ron had left earlier that morning for Columbia, SC. Ron had insisted on taking her to this spot in the Vista, since she claims every time she comes to Augusta she's stressed out with business. So at the moment Teresa and Deamon occupied their hotel room.

"Baby, it's almost one o'clock!" She yelled at the bathroom door.

"I'm coming," he replied before opening the door and adding, "if your ass wasn't trying to put that thing on me, we would've been out of here!"

"I didn't hear your ass complaining twenty minutes ago!" She retorted as she flounced toward him.

"See how you acting, that's why we late now," he protested as he reached for the clothes she'd bought him.

Everything she had purchased, from jumpsuit to the shoes and socks, had the *Jordan* insignia imprinted somewhere.

"So, you're saying that you didn't like it?" She demanded to know as she grabbed his dick through the towel he had wrapped around his waist.

"Na'll, what I'm saying is the total opposite," he clarified while easing away from her and adding, "but if we keep this up, we won't get nothing done."

48

"You do have a point, so next time just get dressed in the bathroom and we won't have this problem."

Ten minutes later they were in Toya's car on their way to pick him up a cell-phone.

"Deamon, are you cool with all of this?" She asked after turning down the sounds of Lauryn Hill.

"All of what?"

"Me and you and how we are together like this?"

He looked over at her and saw the second doubtful expression he'd seen since she arrived. The first was when he stepped to the car the night before, when she obviously knew she was wrong for popping up the way she did.

He wanted to let her know that he felt that they were moving too fast. He also wanted to fill her in about Surina and the way she made him feel. He wanted to tell her that he really felt she was no different from Surina. He wanted to tell her that loyalty to an individual who shows you love, only shows genuine respect to a relationship. He also wanted to let her know that he could never put his full trust in her, because of her past decisions. Not to dwell on her past, but to only think of his future.

49

But when she opened the door for any of this to be said, the only words that came out of his mouth were, "I'm good with it right now. I can't see anything that I can complain about."

"Now that's definitely not what I was expecting to hear!" She stressed with a disturbed expression before adding, "But I guess I can go for that, for now anyway."

They both were silent for a moment before he implied, "You know mom-dukes, and the rest of the family, is going out of town tonight."

"And?"

"And, I wouldn't mind waking up next to you in the morning," he implied as they pulled in front of a *T mobile* building.

She wore a huge grin as she cut the car off and stated, "Just get out so we can get this phone."

****

"Say Black, where the hell is Red at?" The stocky one called Hamburger asked.

"Man, ain't no telling," the taller dark one with the menacing appeal replied.

Hamburger and Black sat on the porch of 1122 Summer Street with grave looks of disgust. After a long night of hustling, they were awakened by the sounds of *Micheal Jackson's*, "Care About Us".

"Man, I know ain't nobody put that shit on but Red!" Black angrily stated.

"Yeah, and the fool had the nerve to leave it on repeat too," Burger confirmed before pulling on a blunt and adding, "I was gonna kick in the door, but you know how that fool get."

He then passed the blunt to Black before Black pointed towards the supermarket across the street and stated, "Now look who's coming."

Red walked from the parking-lot towards the porch with a case of beer in hand, smiling from ear to ear.

When these three smiled all you could see were gold fronts. They were only a quarter of the original family that hustled together. Besides these three, there were the two brothers, Bad-Azz and Hammah, Pimp, Big Ox, Georgia Slim, Rip, Gunslanga and Kruger.

Together they represented a force that was invincible, but at the time the two brothers were incarcerated. Bad-Azz was trapped in Baton Rouge on a federal hold and two attempted murders on police officers, while Hammah was locked-up in Leisburg State Prison serving a fifteen year sentence for aggravated assault.

Together they achieved a lot. Their trust only grew stronger as their trials and tribulations piled up. Their foundation was strong because of their loyalty and respect towards each other. They all knew that without those two virtues, they really stood for nothing.

As far as street credentials, they were known for going all out about theirs. If you knew anything about the streets of Augusta, you knew of the Summer.

"Say Red," Black was the first to confront him, "what you thinking about playing that bullshit early this morning like that!"

"Just what the song say big homie, they don't really care about us," he replied before passing them both a beer and adding, "sometimes we just gotta keep that mind frame."

He placed the rest of the beer in the cooler, that sat next to Hamburger, before stressing to himself, "Dam, we need more ice."

"Na'll, what we need is for your ass to turn that noise off in that room!" Hamburger stressed.

Black just laughed before stating, "If you ask me, it's better than waking up to Purple Rain."

"Man, who the hell is that?" Hamburger asked after seeing a burgundy Mazda pull in front of the house with a Chathum county tag.

"I can't call it," Black replied with a dumbfounded expression.

"Say Butler!" Red called out, "Come out here for a second."

Now Butler was just what his name meant, the door man. It was his job to make sure the house was safe and secure at all times. He had a habit, which just happened to be smoking crack, so his thirst for the drug kept the fellas on their toes.

"Yeah," Butler responded as he walked down the hall towards the front door of the boarding house.

The boarding house consisted of five bedrooms, one bathroom, the kitchen and the front and back porches. The front door was secured with a security gate and behind that was a heavy wood door and a four foot long two by four.

Butler had managed to secure a foot long two by four in the door and one on the floor. He then placed the four foot long two by four between them both. So, if you was thinking of just kicking the door down after you had yanked the steel cage off, you were still in for a big surprise.

"You know that car?" Red asked Butler after seeing him at the gated door.

"No, but do you want me to go see who it is?" He requisitioned with a smile, knowing that he could get a nice blast for the deed.

"Hold up, somebody getting out," Black implied.

After seeing who had stepped out of the car, Hamburger was the first to smile showing his eighteen gold fronts, "What's up playboy?"

"Man, I thought you had done forgot about the Summer," Red added.

"Now picture that!" Kruger responded with a wide grin.

"Where you been homie?" Black asked as he walked down the steps and embraced Kruger with Hamburger and Red following suit.

"Man, the parole board surprised me with this monitor on my leg when I reported," he responded before lifting his pant leg to show them.

"Hell for a hustler, huh?" Red practically stressed.

"Yeah, I guess you can say that," Kruger replied before adding, "but pass me one of them brews."

"Shouldn't you be out looking for a job or something?" Hamburger sarcastically implied.

"He don't need know job, he Jordan down to the socks," Black exposed.

Kruger just chuckled before replying with, "My shortie copped this for me playboy, but where everybody else at?"

"Rip left this morning to take a shower, but he should be back in a few," Hamburger assured.

"Slim and Ox probably across the street getting some rest. You know they got rooms in that boarding house," Red revealed as he pointed to the boarding house across the street.

"Gunslanga somewhere around here trying to make a million off a quarter ounce, and ain't no telling where Pimp at," Black added.

"Pimp probably somewhere with one of these around the way girls," Red stressed causing all of them to burst out laughing.

"But what's really popping with you Mr. Kruger?" Hamburger asked with a sly grin.

"Yeah, how long they got you trapped with

55

that brace?" Red added.

"It ain't nothing but ninety days."

"So you got ninety days to lay back at mom-dukes crib?" Hamburger implied.

"Only time will tell if I'll be doing any relaxing," Kruger replied right before he took a deep gulp of his beer.

"Who that driving, Surina?" Black challenged with a sly grin.

"Hell na'll playboy!" He retorted with a disgusted expression, "That's my shortie from Savannah."

"Yeah, I heard Surina messing with that cat Jimmy from the county anyway," Black revealed.

"You know, it really be tripping me out how these broads be switching up from the real to these lames," Red added.

"You know Jimmy getting a little money, so you know how that shit go," Black stressed.

"I believe that was her that rung the door-bell last night, but me and ole girl was kind of busy," Kruger disclosed.

"And where were the preacher and his wife?" Hamburger insisted to know with a sly grin.

"Bible study!" He replied with a smile causing the rest of them to burst out laughing.

"But on the real though," Kruger added, "I just stopped by to give ya'll my number so ya'll can hit me up from time to time."

"Dam playboy, you ain't gonna introduce us to your shortie?" Black questioned.

"She must be ugly or something?" Hamburger implied.

Kruger just smiled with a look of confidence before waving her over and saying, "Ya'll already know how I get down."

They could hear Lauryn Hill singing about how everything was everything, as she stepped out of the car. From the look on their faces she was far from being ugly.

To her, they were a bunch of hoodlums dressed in Dickies and Timberlands with thermals draped over their wide frames. But she really wasn't concerned with them, her main concern was Deamon, and whether or not he was trying to recapture his past. And if so, which one of his self-proclaimed brothers had Eddie Butler genes.

"Yes boo," is how she responded as she walked up to him.

"These are my peoples, Red, Burger and Black," he stated as he wrapped his arms around her from behind.

"Hello, how are ya'll doing?" She asked with a light smile.

They all nodded their heads, but Black was the first to speak, "We just wanted to thank you for looking out for our little bra like you did."

"Yeah, that's what's good!" Red added, "It's already hell being in the belly of the beast, so you was like an angel sent to help ease his pain."

"Well, since they done hogged all the good stuff to say, where your sister at?" Hamburger stressed causing everyone to burst out laughing.

After everyone calmed down she replied with, "Thanks for the kind greeting, but I have ya'll know that it was Deamon who was there for me when I needed him. But as far as the sister, I only wish I had one for you Burger."

"Well find me a cousin or something with them green eyes!" Hamburger replied causing everyone to burst out laughing again.

She just blushed before Kruger playfully covered her face and said, "On that note fellas, we out."

As he led her back to the car he added, "Ya'll make sure you hit me up later."

****

Surina sat across from Jimmy at the mahogany table in silence. She was really starting to get to him because she'd been that way most of the day.

"So what's up with you?" He asked, taking her out of the trance, "I thought you wanted to come to Red Lobster."

She just looked down into her plate before replying, "I'm sorry Jimmy, I just have a few things on my mind."

"So we done got to the point where you can't talk to me now?" He asked in a frustrated manner.

That's when she finally looked up at him and saw the hurt in his eyes. She knew that the way she was acting toward him was totally out of character, but at the moment it really didn't matter. She wanted to let him know what really had her in a frenzy, but she knew that he wouldn't understand, so she hit him with another excuse.

59

"Jimmy, you know how my grandma be acting," is what finally escaped from her lips.

He just shook his head before stating, "I been telling you that we need to get our own crib anyway. Then maybe I wouldn't have to see you look so frustrated."

"And I've told you before, that I just can't make that call right now."

She had actually received a phone call from her best friend saying that Deamon had come into *T mobile* and purchased a phone with another woman.

From all the letters she received from him while he was incarcerated, she knew that he still had feelings for her. She was just so caught up in her activities with Jimmy that she never made time to respond.

Despite her relationship with Jimmy, there was no doubt in her mind that she wanted Deamon back. Her only real intentions of dealing with Jimmy was to get Deamon off her mind. He was truly the only man that she really loved.

"Surina, are you alright?" Jimmy asked with a genuine look of concern.

"Not really, I don't feel too good," she replied

while raising from her seat and adding, "do you think that you can take me home?"

He raised from his seat and reached in his pocket. After pulling out a fifty dollar bill and placing it on the table he asked her, "Do you need me to take you to the hospital?"

"No, I don't think that it's that serious. I just want to go home and lay down."

The ride home was even quieter than when they were in the restaurant.

After pulling in her grandmother's driveway he asked, "Are you sure you're gonna be alright?"

"Yeah, I just need to get some rest, but I'll call you first thing in the morning," she replied before leaning over and kissing him on the cheek.

When she entered the house she went straight to her room and called her best friend, Deidra.

Deidra was the daughter of the head homicide detective, so she pretty much was able to get away with murder. She had been in more run-ins with the law then Darryl Strawberry and Bobby Brown combined, but with the help of her father she never really got penalized.

Deidra was known as a tomboy while

growing up because of her will to fight whomever. One of the main reasons that Surina befriended her was her ability to fight. They'd had their fair share of squabbles with other girls and that only seem to bring them closer over the years, with a little of each other rubbing off on them both.

"Deidra," Surina was stressing through the receiver.

"What up girl?" She replied.

"Nothing really, just been stressed out."

"So, what's on your mind?" Deidra asked.

"Deamon," is all Surina could utter out.

"I kind of figured that," Deidra confessed, "and the way that he was looking the other day, I can't blame you."

"Yeah, I can only imagine," Surina replied in a sorrowful manner.

"You mean you haven't seen him yet?"

"I only wish I could," she replied, "I've been by his house, twice, and he didn't come to the door either time. I knew his ass was there the last time, cause I could hear the music playing in the backroom. Besides, Tamika told me that he's on the leg monitor, so his ass can't go nowhere."

"Well, he was with that girl at *T mobile*, so that can't be all the way true." Deidra implied before asking, "Do you want me to call him and tell him that you need to see him?"

"I don't really know, hell, he's been dodging me every since he's been home."

"Girl, he's just playing hard to get," she rebutted, "I'm gonna call his ass and let him know what's up."

"Alright, but make sure that you tell him that I have something for him."

"Yeah girl, you know I got you," Deidra stated before she hung the phone up.

After going through her purse, she came up with his number. The phone rang four times before he answered.

"Speak now or forever hold yours," is how he answered.

"Is that how the preacher taught you to answer the phone?" She asked with a light giggle.

"Who this?" He asked.

"This Deidra," she replied while trying to contain her giggles.

"Deidra?" He asked in confusion, "You

talking about the police daughter, Deidra?"

"Yeah, I guess that's me," is all she could respond with.

"Girl, how did you get this number?"

"I guess you don't remember me being the one selling you the phone, huh?" She replied.

"Ain't this against company policy or something?" He jokingly questioned.

"Yeah and no, it all depends on who you are," she responded with authority.

"So what's up, Ms. Above The Law?"

"Surina say that she wants to see you."

The phone was silent for a moment before he replied with, "Look Deidra, I know that's your girl and all, but you need to let her know that I don't wanna see her. Besides, doesn't she have a nigga?"

Before he had realized it, he'd exposed too much emotions and concern on the subject, so now he was dreading it. Showing too many feelings on matters he had no control over was something he was striving to refrain from, especially when those feelings had anything to do with Surina.

"She says that she has something for you,"

Deidra rebutted.

"She ain't got shit that I want! Hell she done had two years to send whatever she wanted to give me, now her time up."

"I guess you're right," Deidra found herself saying, "she was dead wrong for not answering any of your letters."

"Yeah," he agreed, "but all of that is in the past and I've let that be. Maybe you need to tell your friend that it's time for her to do the same."

"Well, I'll tell her," she replied before pausing for a moment and asking, "so do you have company?"

"Na'll, why?" He questioned with a wide grin.

"I thought that maybe I could come through with a bottle or something," she interjected.

"Oh yeah, what you drinking on?" He curiously asked.

"I know you like *Hennessy*," she responded in a sexy manner.

"I can go for that, but I suggest you leave your friend at the house, or both of ya'll would be at the door knocking all night."

"Oh you don't have to worry about that, because I'll definitely be coming by myself."

"Say no more."

"I guess I'll be seeing you in about a half an hour," she stated before hanging the phone up and calling Surina.

-KRUGER-

Here it is Saturday night and I'm sitting here waiting on Surina's closest friend to come over. I knew that she was digging me back in the day, but I just figured that she never wanted to step on her friend's toes. Now with that said, I wonder what has her crossing that line now.

If she wasn't so thugged out, she could've easily got it back then. And if I was gonna cross that line with Surina, I didn't wanna play it that close. But with things the way they are now, I ain't sparing none of these broads out here.

Besides, I have to admit, Deidra really was looking real scrumptious when I saw her the other day. The years have really been good to her.

My mama and the rest of the family are still out of town and I ain't expecting them back until tomorrow night. They at some type of church event in Charlotte doing them, so it's only right that I do me.

Last night was major love for a playa. All my peoples came through to holler and wish me well, even that always too busy cat Gunslanga. You know with all my closest comrades stopping through, you know I had to pull out the camera to send some flicks to Hammah and Bad Azz.

Teresa has to go to work in the morning, so her, Toya and Ron left earlier. I guess bra kind of falling for ole girl, but only time will tell how much they really feeling each other.

Teresa been calling me every since they left. She keep hitting me with Deamon this and Deamon that. Deamon have you ate yet? What did you eat? Dam baby-girl! But, I guess I gotta take it how it comes, especially since I let things ride the way that I have. I know that I'm going against my better judgment, so I guess the best thing to do is try to keep my distance.

Now here I am awaiting this Deidra episode. You know the only real reason I'm going through the motions, is to get back at Surina. I mean, it ain't like I'm thirsty for no ass or something. Yeah, I know it sounds childish, but hell, it is what it is. I ain't trying to take nothing from Deidra, because she is definitely holding her own.

To tell the truth I'm kind of surprised that she's actually coming through. I mean, I know plenty of cats that's been trying to get at her for the longest, but from my understanding, she always brushed them off. Matter of fact, I can't think of one dude that really can say that he's been there. With that said, it's really on!

This must be her at the door.

"Who is it?" I asked as I walked towards the door.

"Who are you expecting?" Is how she replied with that sassy ass mouth.

"You alone?" I asked as I looked through the peep hole.

"No, I have this bottle with me."

I couldn't help but smile as I opened the door, "You know you almost got left out here with all that playing."

She returned my smile with one of her own before replying with, "I guess I'll have to show you just how much I appreciate you not leaving me out in the cold."

Now this wasn't the Deidra that I was

accustomed to seeing in school, in church or even with Surina. This Deidra was straight up stunning.

"I hope that it's alright that I parked in the backyard?" Is what she asked as she brushed up against me.

"That's cool," is all I could respond with as I closed and locked the door.

As I led her towards the kitchen I just had to ask, "So what makes Ms. Deidra wanna spend time with me?"

"Now don't act as if you don't know," she replied as she took her coat off.

Baby girl wore a black mini-skirt that fitted as if it was tailored made. The grey and black sweater she wore exposed the fact that her c- cups was just waiting to be set free. It amazed me how clear and beautiful her walnut complexion was. I really couldn't believe that this sexy ass woman in front of me with these high heels on, was Deidra.

"You already know that I've been digging you for a minute," is what she added as she took a seat at the kitchen table.

"What about Surina?" I just had to ask.

"What about her?" She cross-examined with an offended expression.

"I mean, does she know that you're over here?" I continued to interrogate.

"Look, it's really none of her business if I'm over here or over there. I'm my own woman," she sternly pointed out with a sly grin.

"I can definitely see where you're coming from," I replied right before I grabbed two glasses and filled them up with ice.

"So where your mama them at?"

"Out of town," I responded as I poured us both a glass of cognac.

"So when do you expect them back?"

"Tomorrow night."

"So I have you all to myself the whole night?" She quizzed.

"If you know how to act," I replied as I walked to the fridge to find something we could eat before I asked, "you hungry?"

"Not really."

"Well, I might just order a pizza or something, you cool with that?"

"I can go for that."

It took a little over an hour for the pizza to arrive. By that time we had drunk most of the fifth she'd bought. We talked about any and everything.

You know I usually always watched what I would say to a female whenever we was talking, but with her I was open for any conversation. I mean she really was cool. She surprised me with her view on a lot of things, especially on the issue of loyalty.

"You know that I have some night clothes in the car," is what I heard her imply.

"Do you really think that you're gonna need them?" I asked in sort of a slurred manner.

Now either she didn't notice that I was tipsy or she could really careless as she stood over me while I sat on the couch. My black wife- beater was the first thing she pulled off of me. She then started to kiss and suck all over my neck. With me being me, I took it from there.

From the living room, the kitchen, the bathroom, to finally the bedroom, I had her moaning out my name. Our session was somewhat different from me and Teresa's episodes. The intensity had me so caught up I knew I couldn't just let this be a one night thing. The thing is, I couldn't let her know that I was trying to lock that ass down either.

When she woke me up, to take a shower with her, it was a little after ten in the morning. Man,

Deidra a true beast. The moment we hit the shower she went right back to sucking all over me. When we finally stepped out of the shower, I asked her did her daddy know where she was.

She just smiled at me before revealing, "He's in Charlotte with your mama them."

"Dam you're slick as hell, but I'm kind of digging that."

That's when things got a little serious, well at least the expression on her face did.

"Deamon, you know that there is no limit to the things you can accomplish with me," is what she stated as she eased a little closer.

"It sounds as if you're putting in an application or something."

"It's just a little something to think about."

"And you already know that I'm gonna do just that."

"Well, while you're thinking about that," is what she stressed as she dropped to her knees before adding, "I want you to think about this."

(CHAPTER 3)

"Say Weasel," Jimmy was saying as he drove down James Brown Boulevard.

"Yeah, what up?" He replied with a cloud of smoke seeping from his nose and mouth from the blunt he was smoking.

"You ain't find nothing else about who could've pull that?"

"Man, I wish I did."

"The way I see it, whoever hit us gotta be an older cat or a youngun with some helluva patience."

Weasel contemplated on that for a moment before adding, "Or somebody close to a nigga."

Jimmy smirked at the thought for a moment before agreeing, "I can see where you're coming from."

Three months had passed since they found their stash was missing. They investigated, but nothing ever came to the surface. If these two never really agreed on anything, they now agreed on the fact that whomever was behind the heist definitely knew too much.

"Say playboy, we don't even need to sweat that," Weasel assured, "Whoever it was will soon or later show their hand."

"Yeah, but we been saying that for the longest," Jimmy rebutted, "we done set traps for this nigga and all, but ain't nothing came up."

"That could be a good thing. The way I see it, everybody gets hit at least once, no matter who he is. The only beef I have is not being able to set an example out here!" Weasel stressed with a cold stare.

"But hey, if they got the message without the violence, then cool. I mean, we already know that whoever did it is scared as hell. I mean, they gotta be, wouldn't you be scared?" Jimmy stated causing them both to burst out laughing.

They were just riding around with no real destination. Their business required a lot of attention and persistence, so despite whatever was going on in their personal lives, they knew they couldn't neglect the game. As they rode around they both were concentrating on seeking new clientele, so Weasel suggested that they roll through Summer Street, since he had family out there.

"Who your people out here anyway?"

Jimmy asked as he turned on Summer Street.

"That nigga with the one arm they call Pimp," he replied before seeing a few cats sitting on the porch, "stop right here."

Hamburger was the first person he noticed when he bailed out of the Infiniti.

"What up Lil Weasey," Hamburger greeted before adding, "I thought you wasn't fucking with The Summer no more."

"Na'll Burger!" Weasel rebutted, "Nigga you know that I can never forget the block that paved the way for a hustler."

The two embraced before Weasel finally recognized who the other cat was on the porch.

"Oh shit!" He practically yelled, "Big homie?"

"What up homie?" Kruger replied as he stood up to embrace Weasel.

"When they set you free?"

"Man, I've been home like three months now. I just been on that leg monitor," Kruger replied with a wide grin.

From the looks on their faces, there was no doubt that they were both happy to see each other.

"Playboy, I want you to see something," Weasel expressed as he ran back to the car.

"Dam playboy, I can't believe that you still got that pistol," Kruger declared as Weasel came back cradling a chrome .45.

Weasel kept the gun as a reminder of the bond they shared before Kruger was incarcerated. Kruger had given it to him as a reminder that everything wasn't sweet in the streets.

"Boy, I've been hearing good things about you out here," Kruger stressed.

"You know I've been doing alright for myself, but you know we can all be doing better," he replied with a smile before asking, "why don't you bend a few corners with a playa?"

"I wish I could, but I have a few things to take care of myself, and there go my ride right there," he revealed with a head nod towards the dark blue Honda that had pulled in front of Jimmy's car.

"Here go my number, make sure you hit me," Kruger added after grabbing a pen and notebook out of the chair next to him.

"I'll hit you up first thing in the morning, since I see you gonna be with Deidra all night," was his response after grabbing the piece of paper.

"Dam bra, the county got you out here hating like that?" Kruger questioned before turning to Hamburger and saying, "Make sure you take care of my jealous hearted little bra here, and hit me up if anything pops off."

After embracing them both he said, "Make sure you hit me up Mr. Jealousy," before hopping in the car with Deidra.

After seeing the Honda pull off Weasel turned to Hamburger and said, "The nigga had Surina and now he got Deidra?"

"You already know how that nigga do," Hamburger affirmed as he stepped off the porch to make a sale.

"Where the rest of the fellas at?" Weasel asked as Hamburger walked on the side of the house with the fiend.

"It's Friday, so you know they probably down the street at Charlie's," he replied as he kept his eyes focused on the street.

"Well, here is my number so that ya'll can get some of these sweet ass prices," he declared as he wrote down the number on the pad.

Jimmy was on the phone when Weasel hopped back in the car.

"Yeah that fool just stepped back in," Jimmy stated through the receiver as he pulled off, "yeah, I'm gonna let him know," he added before hanging up.

"Let me know what?" Weasel questioned as he rolled another blunt.

"Nothing really, Tom-Tom just wants us to stop through his crib in the morning to pick up another pack. Oh yeah, he say he got some hydro for you too."

"Now that's my peoples right there," Weasel stressed with a wide grin.

"Yeah whatever, but wasn't that Deidra who just pulled off?" Jimmy asked.

"Yeah, that was her. She supposes to be fucking with my nigga, Kruger. You know that's the same dude I told you gave me this pistol," he stated while holding the pistol up.

"Yeah, the one you say help you get on your feet."

"Yeah, that's him," Weasel reveal with a grin before adding, "you know he also the same nigga that popped Surina's cherry."

"Oh yeah," Jimmy replied while trying to conceal his jealousy.

78

"Yeah, and now the nigga got her best friend, now tell me that ain't a smooth muthafucka?" Weasel stated while shaking his head, "Man I've been trying to get that pussy for the longest, but here he is just stepping out and she just throws him the pussy."

"Now how you know that he ain't go after her?" Jimmy asked.

"He don't get down like that. Playboy just sits back and let them come to him."

"So he a true playa, huh?"

"If you ask me, he a true hustler first."

"So you gonna put him down or what?"

"That all depends on you," Weasel stated before firing up the blunt and adding, "being that him and Surina done kicked it, I figured that you might not be too comfortable with that."

Jimmy looked over at him and couldn't help but smile. He was just wondering how Weasel was going to handle the situation, so it eased him after hearing what he just said.

"So why they break up?" He asked Weasel.

"From my understanding, they never did, he just got locked-up, and you know how these broads be getting ghost when a soldier get trapped."

79

"Yeah, she told me about that cat, say his name was Deamon."

"Yeah, that's what his mama named him, but the streets know him as Kruger."

"Dam playboy, it's a small world," Jimmy stated with a bewildered expression, "your Kruger and her Deamon, the same dude."

-TERESA-

You know I've been kind of crazy every since Deamon has got off that monitor. It's like I feel he should be with me every day, all day. I just got off the phone with his ass and he's already canceling our little escapade. The excuse he used was the fact that he has to work. I offered to send him some money, but he stressed the fact that's the reason he has a job.

Now that's one of the many reasons I love him to death. I know if it was anybody else, especially someone just getting out like him, they'd probably try to get all they could from a sister. But Deamon, he's that rare brother that actually considers the fact that I have other things to do with my money.

I'm so proud of him. My baby is actually working and has even bought him a car. Him and Ron even have them a nice apartment together. I haven't seen it yet, but me and Toya helped them pick out the furniture. Toya even hooked them up with her discount.

Toya and Ron has gotten just as close as me and Deamon, if not closer. She's even talking about me and her moving to Augusta and getting us a nice condo or something. Hell, I could easily transfer to Augusta Medical Prison, and she says that her job keeps harassing her about the manager position at their Augusta location, so we'll both still have a job.

She's already talked to Ron about it and he's all for it, so it's really all on me and Deamon. To tell the truth, I'm kind of weary of asking him, because I don't want him to feel if I'm crowding him. He's suppose to be here Tuesday, so despite my weariness I'm gonna see what he has to say about it. Hell, I need a change of scenery.

Savannah has really got old to a sister. I mean, look at me. I've just got off work and now I'm stretched out on this old couch sipping on a cheap glass of wine with the 'Waiting to Exhale' soundtrack humming through the speakers. Now tell me that I'm not living a boring life. That's why I need my baby here.

It be tripping me out how he's always acting all hard, like he really ain't feeling me like that over the phone. But, just as soon as he gets in my presence, it's like he can't keep his dam hands off of me. Just like that time he had just got off that monitor.

Him and his brother drove down and kicked it with Toya until I got off work. I had been wondering why he'd been calling me all day with an attitude about nothing. I didn't even know that he was in town, so I dragged through the day no differently then I usually do.

As soon as I pulled up in my apartment complex there his ass was, sitting on that long old grey car. You know, I don't even see how they can still call that a Cadillac.

"Where the hell have you been, you should've been home thirty minutes ago," was the first thing he said to me.

I wasn't about to entertain the irrelevant, so I just walked up to him and practically threw my tongue down his throat. I guess you really don't know how much you really be missing somebody at times. He stayed for the full three days that I was off, so we went to the Crab Shack, Hilton Head and walked through both malls. This nigga literally had me blushing for the next three days.

Toya say that I'm dick whipped, but she obviously don't know what she's talking about. It ain't no secret that he had me way before I got the dick. The dick just put the seal on it.

-KRUGER-

Man, I don't really know how I'm doing it, but everything is moving at a steady pace for me right now. I mean, what can a playa really ask for fresh out of prison?

As of right now, I have a lot going on. For starters, I'm off in this high price ass hotel room with the always ready to do whatever for her man, Deidra. She so down for a playa, it's scary. The only real complaint that I have with her is the fact that we be spending too much on these rooms. You know that shit starts really adding up, getting a room every other night.

I don't think that she knows that me and Ron has an apartment together. The thing about that is, I think I'm more at ease with her not knowing, for now anyway. I mean, with her not knowing, only helps to keep down a lot of confusion, for the time being.

Don't get me wrong, she knows her position and plays it well, considering she knows about Teresa and all. It's just, I feel it's too early to allow those two worlds to bump heads.

Besides Deidra, like I mentioned a moment ago, I'm still caught up on the always too energized, sexy green eyed, Teresa. She's a beast, without a doubt! But she hasn't been living up to any of the things she use to feed me behind that wall. That's just another thumbscrew between us.

Teresa so blind that she thinks that I'm still working at that magazine factory, but the Summer has had my full attention for the past two months. I felt that I was getting pimped by that temp agency, and from the way I was looking at it, I'd already allowed Babylon to pimp me enough behind them walls and gates. But picture me trying to explain that to Teresa.

At this moment I can honestly say that I'm becoming well balanced. Okay, on one side I have Teresa and Deidra, who actually weigh nicely next to each other. Now on the other side, I have nine or ten cats that I can converse with and relate to. I mean, me and my homies are like family, and with that said, I know that I'm blessed.

"In order to be successful, you have to be ready for success itself!" Is what Burger might say to crank up the session.

Being around all these different mind frames is a great advantage out here in these streets. Alot of cats try to do things by themselves out here, which is sort of foolish. We think we're being smart by excluding your only real source of income, which is other people.

I just sent Hammah a money order, so he should be good for a minute. I gotta remind myself to get at Burger to make sure he check on Bad Azz, since them two were closer. My mama and the rest of the family straight too, so like I was saying, everything is on the up and up right now.

The way that I'm looking at it is, as long as I go to bed with more money than I woke up with, I'm making some kind of progress. I have like 3,400 stashed in the Caddy, 460 on me and like 42 grams stashed on the Summer. If I never bought the Caddy, I'd probably be sitting a little better, but it was a nice investment cause every playa needs some transportation.

I know that the nigga Weasel thinks that I'm gonna fool with him, but I really can't see us collaborating, being the right move. He rolling with ole boy, and I know he's going to be tripping about that broad, so it's best I just let them be.

"Deamon, what's wrong with you boo?" Deidra asked after turning over and seeing that I was up.

"It ain't nothing, I'm just pondering over a few things."

She rose out of bed and headed towards the bathroom.

Right before she walked through the bathroom door she asked, "Baby, what was Jimmy them doing down on the Summer?"

"Minding their business!" I harshly replied.

"I'm just saying," she pointed out in a pleading manner, "you really don't need to be messing with them, cause they draw too much heat."

The look on her face was sincere, so I knew that she was only speaking from the heart. The thing with that is, I have never been comfortable discussing street endeavors with anyone, let alone a women, unless she getting money with me. But, I'm not so foolish that I won't see what she knows.

"So baby-girl, what is really up with Weasel and his man?" I asked as she was climbing back in the bed.

"All I know is, somebody broke in Jimmy's car and stole a nine ounces a couple of months ago and they never found out who did it. They thought Pimp did it, since his mama stay down the street from Jimmy's mama. That's the only reason I asked about them."

I was about to ask her where she'd learned all this, but the answer hit me before I could even utter it out. And being the person that I am, what's understood doesn't need to be talked about. So I just ended up staring at the ceiling in silence.

"I know that you still love her," I heard her practically whisper.

Now I knew that this would sooner or later come up, so I wasn't too surprised.

"Look Deidra, my love ain't got shit to do with her, and you should know that by now," I revealed without even looking in her direction. "I'm sure that you've read some of them letters that I wrote her, so yeah I did love her. But her violation turned out to be alot bigger than love itself, so me and her could never be an item again."

"You have to realize," I continued, "that neither one of us is promised tomorrow, so I couldn't help but respect her wishes. But believe me, now has come the time where she has to respect mine. Life is way too short for a playa to be going backwards, so I gotta keep it moving."

"It still sounds to me as if you want her back," she stated as if she was worried that I was going to leave her.

I sat there for a moment and allowed what she'd just said to soak in. Then I realized that I was looking at the situation in the wrong aspect. I never really considered, until now, what she was more than willing to sacrifice just to be laying next to me.

I then reached over and kissed her on the forehead before saying, "I'm content with what I'm working with right now, so ole girl is your least worry."

After she rested her head on my chest I added, "This is a me and you thing, and it can really have a beautiful ending, you just gotta believe in us."

****

Jimmy was sleeping like a baby as Surina stared down at him. He'd been through a lot in the last few hours so he was far past exhausted. The combination of Kruger and Deamon started it all, followed by a huge argument with Surina. He practically smoked and drunk himself to the state of oblivion so it was nothing for Surina to give in and put him to sleep.

As she glared down at him she still couldn't believe what Jimmy had just told her. She never thought that Deidra could actually betray her like she was. The entire time she never blamed Deamon, because she knew that he was only getting back at her for not staying in touch.

It bothered her more that she didn't see it coming. She felt that no-one knew how he operated better than she did, so she figured all she had to do is talk to him and eventually everything would work out in her favor.

Deidra had told her that she was going to Atlanta, but now she knew why she never ask her to go. Deidra had deceived and betrayed her and she was going to make sure she paid for it.

A tear fell down her cheek as she thought about all of the plans that she shared with Deidra about her and Deamon's future. Surina actually felt that she'd helped bring the woman out of Deidra, only to have her use those same skills to take away the one person whom she truly loved.

"I hate that bitch!" She exclaimed with disgust.

She then took a few deep breaths and whispered, "Calm down Surina. Girl you know he don't love her."

After she thought about it a moment, she came to the conclusion that he was only playing Deidra. The way she looked at it, she was just going to let Deidra play herself. In her mind, she knew that she had more to offer then Deidra would ever have. Besides, she had an ace in the hole for his homecoming gift.

Surina knew with him being back on Summer Street, and her having what she had for him, they'd be together in due time. In her mind, her only real stumbling block was Jimmy.

She knew that she loved him, but she was in love with Deamon. Jimmy had been nothing but good to her so she didn't want to hurt him. With that thought in mind, at the moment, leaving him wasn't an option.

At that moment she got on her knees and started praying to GOD to work everything out for everyone, with Deamon back in her life.

****

It was Sunday, around two in the evening and all the fellas were sitting around the table eating in Ryan's steakhouse. It took three tables to accommodate the nine man cartel, who were being served by twin sisters. They sat in the back of the restaurant with Hamburger in the only position to see the buffet area.

"Say Pimp," Kruger called out to get his attention from the chicken wing he was eating.

"What's up playboy?" Pimp replied.

Now Pimp was the sore thumb of the cartel. If you looked at him with the naked eye, you would think that he was less fortunate, because of him being born with one arm. But he was the only one arm cat in the city of Augusta with a dozen gold fronts in his mouth. It also didn't help the fact that his neck and left arm was filled with gold.

"You know the word is that you was the prime suspect in that lost that Weasel and Jimmy took a while back," Kruger announced.

"Yeah, I heard," he replied before adding, "Weasel got at me about that, but it wasn't me, I wish it was though."

91

"You got that shit right," Georgia Slim added, "The way shit been going, that would've been the move to give us that boost to get where we need to be."

Georgia Slim wore a huge gold rope with a superman medallion around his neck. Everyone on Summer Street invested in one. To them it was a symbol of what they were together, invincible.

"Say Kruger," Hamburger pried while licking his fingers, "what up with your girl in Savannah?"

"She chillen," he responded in between bites of his steak and bake potato, "I'm suppose to ride up there Tuesday to spend a few days with her, so I should be back before Friday."

"You might as well stay up there until Saturday, so you can hit that club Frozen up," Red suggested.

"I would, but it just ain't my time for no club scene. I gotta have at least seven or eight stacks first," he replied with a serious expression.

"So, who was riding with you?" Gunslanga asked.

"I'm solo."

"Well, I might ride with you, cause I have a few things to take care of in the Sea-Port. We can even take the Lincoln, because I know that you ain't really ready to push that Lac like that."

"That's what's up," Kruger replied with a smile.

Rip and Big Ox was talking about hitting the bowling alley later, while Black was talking to one of the twin waitresses when Weasel walked over to the table.

"What up brethren?" He greeted as he grabbed a seat and pulled it to their table.

"Dam playboy, how did you know that we were here?" Black asked him.

"Dam brother Black, I use to be on the Summer too. Beside, everybody knows that if Hamburger ain't on the porch on Sunday, he's at the nearest buffet," he replied causing everyone to burst out laughing.

"I guess you have a point there cuz," Pimp stated before adding, "but he said you came through looking for us yesterday, so what's really good?"

"Twenty-eight, uncut for the six hundred," he announced with a sly grin.

"Well, let me get six for thirty-four," Kruger challenged.

STUCK

"No problem big homie," he replied before adding, "and since it's you, I'll even throw in an extra one. Count it as a welcome home present."

"That's the business!" Kruger stressed, "So when you ready?"

"Bra, I done paid for my food, so let me eat first, then we can get right at it," he responded as he raised from his seat.

"Say Weasel, I might need to grab a few of them myself," Gunslanga revealed.

"It don't matter, but those prices is only for ya'll, I'm taxing everybody else eight," he stated before he walked towards the buffet.

-KRUGER-

"What up playboy, you about ready?" Slanga was asking me.

"Yeah, I'm ready," I replied with before implying, "I guess we'll take a shower when we get there?"

"It ain't but one o'clock, so you still have time to get one in if you wanna," he inquired.

I looked at him and realized that he needed

94

one too, and this fool takes all day to wash up, so we really ain't got that kind of time.

"Na'll playboy," I stressed while shaking my head, "we both a just take one when we get there."

It had been thirty seven hours of straight grinding. Me, Slim, Burger, Rip, and Black held the trap down.

After I copped that little bit from Weasel, I cooked up five and put the other two up with the little bit I already had. I call myself holding them down for a rainy day. With those five, I brought back eight and some change. With only one quarter ounce sale, I only have four and a half left. So I made my money back and a extra 650 in that short time.

"Say Slanga," I called as we were getting in the Continental, I need to stop by the crib to drop something off."

"Yeah whatever," he replied before pulling off.

Now Slanga caught his name from his trigger happy days. He was hustling on Miller Street with his cousin Ronnie. One day a few haters ambushed Ronnie in his trap and robbed him for a quarter brick, four stacks and his life.

It was an automatic war on the streets of

Augusta and Slanga was determined to win it. After filling a few cats with holes and beating a body case he calmed down and got about his money. Since then he's relocated on the Summer. He didn't grind out of the same house as us, his trap house was actually located down the street, closer to Dyess Park.

He had his cousin Prime and some female name Kay-Kay hustling for him when he wasn't there. He just did three and some change his-self, so me and him had a lot in common.

"What you about to drop off?" He asked as he pulled in the parking lot of my apartment building.

"Some of this bread," I responded, "I ain't trying to take too much down there."

"You might wanna bring that with you," he suggested, "I might can get some better numbers threw at us down there. How much you working with anyway?"

"I ain't got but four stacks."

"Put 500 more with that and you might can get a quarter," he stressed before adding, "I would've told you earlier, but everybody ain't gotta know what we do."

"Let's ride then."

It took us a little over two hours to get there. I guess you can blame it on the deep conversation we was having, but whatever it was, it brought us closer. To me, he was just a taller and older mirror image of myself. We were two young cats taking risk every day, with hopes of a better tomorrow.

"Say Slanga, what up with that broad Kay-Kay?" I asked as he drove down Abercorn.

"Shortie straight, but I got her to strictly get that money for a playa," was all he revealed to me.

"True," was all I thought to say.

I mean he said what he said, even though I thought I saw something different. See Kay-Kay been sending messages through smokers saying she wanna get at me. The only reason that I never responded was the fact that I didn't know where her and my homie stood. But since he ain't pressed the issue, I guess she's open for fornication.

Kay-Kay is this sexy pecan-tan shortie with hazel eyes and a body like Halle Berry. Her attitude could've been measured to the gangster level of the rapper Boss. With all that said, there wasn't a doubt in my mind that I wanted to sample her unseen qualities.

97

"What time does your girl get off work?" He asked as we pulled in the *La'Quinta Inn*.

"Like four, but she already know to hit me up when she gets off."

"Well, I'm gonna call my peoples so we can meet up later. It's almost four now, so you want me to drop you at her crib or something?"

"Na'll, I'm a chill here at the room and let her come scoop me up, you just make sure you check on that."

"Playboy, that's a done deal, you just make sure you keep your phone on," he responded as we walked in the room.

Teresa called while I was in the shower, so Slanga answered my phone. He says that she was on her way over. I threw on the *Polo* gear that she had coped me a few weeks ago. Just as I was tying up my Air Max's, she was bamming on the door.

"You know it's bad enough that you're knocking on this door like you the police, but you have to be dressed like one too," is what Slanga stressed to her after opening the door.

"Hello to you too, Mr. Gunslanga," was her sarcastic remark.

I just burst out laughing as I walked passed

him out the door.

"You just make sure you take care of my bra," is what he stressed right before he closed the door behind us.

She lightly pushed me to the wall and forced her tongue down my throat.

"Tell me that you miss me!" She practically demanded the moment our lips separated.

"I see that you ain't giving me much time to tell you nothing," is how I replied as I slid a few inches away and added, "I guess we ain't going nowhere tonight."

"I wasn't planning on to," is what I heard as she attempted to fill that small space I'd just created, "unless you have some place else you'd rather be?"

"I tell you what, let's get you home and we'll discuss it after we get you clean," I responded as I led her to the car.

As soon as we stepped in her apartment, I went straight for the tub and started her bath water. While the water was running, I went to snatch her up.

She was in her laundry room putting a load of clothes in the washing machine, so I grabbed her from behind and pecked her on the neck. She had her hair pinned up, so I let it down right before I led her to the bathroom.

"So, Mr. Hard Ass Deamon can actually give a woman a bath?" She asked with a sarcastic smile as I turned the water off.

"You'll be surprised of what I can do," I replied with as I was taking her clothes off.

Before she stepped in the tub I asked her, "Do you have some special oils or something that you put in your water?"

She just shook her head and stepped in.

See a playa really just can't take the initiative and put all type of oils and beads in a woman's water, because all of their bodies aren't the same. Some are allergic to certain things, and believe it or not some woman catch yeast infections with certain oils or beads, so the smart thing to do is ask first.

"Towels and wash clothes?" I asked her before she pointed towards the hall closet.

After washing every part of her body, with a little extra attention in the places unseen, I instructed her to step out of the tub before I dried her off. Her body is almost flawless, and the only reason I'm saying almost is the fact that I feel no-one is flawless.

I gently scooped her up and carried her into her bedroom. After I placed her on the bed, I grabbed her baby-oil and massaged every inch of her, with a little fondling here and there to set her body aflame.

During this period, neither of us spoke a word. It was like we was acting out a part in a movie or something. And as far as I was concerned, we both were playing our parts to perfection.

I raised up and made my way towards the front door to see if it was locked. After making sure the house was secure, I started to strip as I made my way back to her.

I then climbed over her as she laid on her stomach before I heard her say, "I thought you was about to leave me."

I could actually hear her body calling out for the attention that I knew it longed for, in her voice.

"And leave your fine ass here so that somebody else can come finish what I started?" Is what I responded with a smirk as I turned her over to gaze in those dazzling green eyes.

This woman was too much. When I stared down into her face the only two words that came to mind was, "Simply beautiful!"

After forty-five minutes of slow and intense bumping and grinding we both found ourselves in a state of hibernation.

-TERESA-

I don't care what nobody say, I got the finest nigga around here sleeping in my bed right now. I'm really tripping because it has been times that I be alone in this same bed just wishing he was right where like he is now. He said that he just got off work, so I'm a let him rest. Besides, he put in enough work for it.

I really need to get my butt up and cook something, cause I know that he's gonna be hungry when he wakes up. He don't eat pork, so the only thing I can really cook is chicken. Yeah, I can try some chicken and fix some mash potatoes and corn, that's simple enough.

Dam, there go that dam phone.

"Hello," I stressed after picking up the phone.

"What up girl?" Is what I hear Toya ask.

"What's up Toya?" I calmly replied.

"Is prince charming there yet?"

"Yeah, but he's resting right now."

"Dam, you don't waste no time do you?" She sarcastically asked with a light giggle.

"Why should I?" I replied with a giggle of my own, "You already know that we have to make the best of these long distant relationships when we can."

"I can definitely feel you on that," she replied before pausing for a moment and questioning, "but guess what?"

"What?"

"I'm pregnant!" She revealed.

Now I really didn't know if she was overjoyed or depressed, so I asked her, "What did he say?"

"I didn't tell him yet," she answered as if she wasn't sure she was going to tell him.

"When did you find out?" I asked.

"This morning," she replied before pausing for a second and adding, "you already know what I'll usually do in this situation, but I'm thinking about keeping this one."

I couldn't help but smile at the thought of

Toya having a baby.

"What about Eddie?" I just had to ask because I know how she feels about him.

"I'll write him a letter or something. Hell, I can't just sit here and wait for him forever," she confessed in a saddened tone.

"I ain't trying to be funny or nothing, but you know that I've been telling you that for a minute."

"Yeah, you have, but I'm going to let you get back to your man, I just wanted you to know," is what she insisted as if I had spoiled her mood.

"Alright, but call me if you need anything," I managed to get out before she hung up.

I was about to call her back and curse her ass out for hanging up on me like that, but I knew I had brought it on myself. She called me to get words of encouragement and I shot her down, so calling her back would only make matters worse, so it's really best I just let her be.

Deamon is really going to flip when he hear this. Hell, I want a baby too. I wonder what me and his baby would look like. After the session we just had, I'll be surprised if I'm not pregnant.

If it's a girl we can name her Demetria, but if it's a boy he'll just be a junior. Listen to me, I'm already naming kids and I don't even know if I'm pregnant yet. I need to get my ass up and start cooking.

Here I am talking about cooking, hell, I need to get my ass up and take a dam shower.

After a twenty minute shower, I stepped back in the bedroom and here his ass on the phone talking to some girl. I don't know who she is, but she's loud as hell. I really can't believe that he has the audacity to be laying off in my bed butt-boogie-ass-naked talking to some bitch on the phone.

I really didn't want to crowd him like that but Lord knows I wasn't about to just sit there and allow him to kick it with her in my bed, so as soon as he hung up with her, I playfully asked, "Dam baby-boy, who are you cheating on me with already?"

Do you believe this fool just started chuckling like what I asked was cute before he replied with, "You need to stop tripping, that was Tamika calling about some family business."

He then raised from out of the bed and grabbed me from behind and seductively asked, "You couldn't wait for me to take a shower with you?"

He think that he can just touch me and everything is alright. Now I'm gonna let that go for now and play the I'm cool role, cause I really don't know if it was her or not, and plus he's touching me in my spot.

"I didn't want to wake you," I stated as I turned to face him, "you looked as if I put that thing on you, so I had to let you rest up for the main event tonight."

"You mean to tell me that it gets better than that?" He questioned as he lightly brushed my face with the back of his fingers.

Dam! Every time this cat touches me I get wetter and wetter.

"Of course," I started to say in a low and lustful tone, "you should know that I have plenty of hot like fire nights for you."

That's when he placed his mouth over mine again. Talk about fireworks! I had to pull away before we found ourselves entangled again.

"I'll cook us something to eat while you take your shower," is what I suggested after I caught my breath.

"Now tell me what I look like letting you cook when you just got off work?" He implied as he made his way towards the bathroom, "Just put some clothes on so we can go out and grab something to eat," is what I heard him add before I heard the bathroom door close.

While he was in the shower I pulled out the clothes that I'd bought him earlier in the week. I got my baby some *Polo*, from the sweatshirt to the socks, he gonna be fly. Maybe I can get him to go to karaoke night at Frozen.

****

Firebug sat in front of the *La'Quinta Inn* in his bronze on bronze '79 Seville with the patience of a hungry lion in search for food. He was a 51 year old hustler who once shared a cell with Gunslanga. He had always told Gunslanga that he would make sure he looked out for him whenever they got out of prison, and he'd kept his word.

Firebug had grown to admire the way Gunslanga carried himself while they were incarcerated. He admired the way he was so attentive when business was at hand, but as he sat there in his Seville, he was heated with his young protégé because he was already fifteen minutes late. What irked him more was the fact that he was parked right next to the Lincoln he'd helped him picked out, but there was no sign of Gunslanga.

Since they'd both made it home and started conducting business together, Firebug had hooked his protégé up with his younger cousin, Amanda. Before he brought the two together, him and Gunslanga would meet up somewhere between the two cities, but now that he'd met someone, he didn't mind driving the full way to Savannah.

Firebug claimed that he joined the two because he felt they were perfect for each other. If it wasn't for their blood relations, Firebug probably would've kept Amanda for himself. She was built just the way he preferred his woman, young, ambitious and a strong determination to get money. All of that trapped inside a figure eight body.

Picking back up his phone Firebug called Gunslanga.

"Yeah," Gunslanga answered.

"Youngblood, where you at?" He practically screamed through the receiver.

"Right behind you Pop, we just pulled in."

Firebug hung his phone up and stepped out the car as he saw them hop out of Amanda's Altima.

"Look Amanda, you need to stop holding him hostage, because it seems to me that he can't play the game and chew gum at the same time," Firebug stressed as he leaned on his car.

"Stop tripping Pop, cause we was here at two, so you the one who really in the wrong," Slanga revealed as he embraced him.

"What I told you about that Pop shit!" He retorted as he lightly pushed him away with a smile before turning to Amanda, "Baby-girl, grab that bag out of the trunk for me."

Gunslanga threw his arm around him, "Come on in before you have a stroke or something."

After stepping in the room Firebug asked, "So where your partner."

"He'll be here in a few, he just called, but he good people though," he replied as Firebug took a seat at the small table in the corner of the room.

"One thing about you young blood, and I might be disrespecting a helluva code with this here, but I trust your judge of character. If you say that he straight, then I believe he straight."

Slanga just smiled before stressing, "Preciate that Pop, that really means a lot."

"So what kind of bread ya'll working with?" Firebug asked.

"I got like eight and I think that he has like four," Gunslanga replied as Amanda and Kruger walked in the room.

"What's going big homie?" Kruger greeted after locking the door behind him.

"Business bra," Gunslanga acknowledged before introducing everyone, "Kruger, this here is Firebug and Amanda, and vice-versa."

"Nice to meet ya'll," Kruger stated as he walked over by Gunslanga.

"Dam youngblood, your mama named you Kruger?" Firebug sarcastically asked.

Kruger just smirked before he replied with, "Na'll, that's just something the streets threw at me."

"Well, Slanga tells me that you wanted to spend a few dollars," Firebug implied as he studied Kruger before adding, "he also say that you're good people, so I'm giving it to you just like I give it to him."

"That's love right there," Kruger replied with a wide grin as he looked over at Gunslanga.

"So what are you trying to spend?"

"Four stacks."

"Well, I can give you a quarter for the four and front you a big eight for the two back."

"Now that's the business!" Kruger stated in an overexcited manner.

"The same goes for you too Slanga. I'll give you a half for the eight and front you a quarter for the four back," Firebug continued as he grabbed the bag from Amanda, "see that's for ya'll won't have to keep coming back and forth, up and down that road."

"Good looking Pop!" Gunslanga excitedly stressed.

"Ya'll just stay focused and stack that paper and it'll be good looking for all of us," he replied as he grabbed the product and the scale out of the bag.

"Slanga, you should be getting one of these on your own on the next trip," he added before handing one of the two kilos to Gunslanga, "and Kruger you should be coping no less than half."

"With prices like this, that definitely won't be a problem," Kruger assured.

Ten minutes later Firebug was pulling out of the hotel's parking-lot with more confidence in his Augusta operation, then he had when he pulled in.

He knew that they were thugs, but he also

felt that they were more of hustlers then anything. But he wasn't so naïve to know that it took both traits to be successful in the game, let alone achieve in the streets.

-KRUGER-

At the moment, me and Slanga on our way back to Augusta with a bag full of coke. It hasn't really dawned on me yet, but I still gotta let this cat know how I feel about this here.

"Say big homie," I stress after turning down the sounds of *Scarface's*, 'Smile For Me', "I really preciate you bringing me in on this here."

"Playboy, everything is all good," is what he replied with after looking over at me, "I brought you in, cause it ain't no way that I can get all this money out here by myself."

"I feel you, but still," I begin to stress before he cut me off.

"I already know playboy, but I feel that you're ready to get this money by any means! But you have to know that by dealing with them cats Weasel and Jimmy ain't gonna do nothing but get us all indicted," he implied before pausing for a moment and adding, "and believe it or not playboy, you'll be the first one to go down, and it'll be all behind that broad."

I definitely could feel where he was coming from, because I'd already sat and contemplated over the same thing. I've been off the street too long to be coming back and getting crossed up behind speculation.

"Playboy, you definitely right about that there," I replied before I questioned his fling, "but what about ole girl Amanda, what's her position?"

He looks over at me with this sly grin for a moment before replying with, "She cool for now, but if it comes a time where she has violated, it's real simple. Just like Snoop Dogg said, "it ain't no pussy good enough to get burnt while I'm up in it!"

"I can definitely feel you on that playboy!" I responded with a light smile knowing that he meant every word he just said.

Truth be told, I feel the same way about Deidra and Teresa. I just hope that neither one of them ever put me in that position.

As far as Teresa is concerned, I'm already knowing that I can't inform her about anything that's going on with me and these streets. That's why when she hit me with that I wanna move to

Augusta scenario, I let her know off the jump that I wasn't feeling it. She screaming that Toya already talked to Ron about it, which I knew was a lie, cause I don't feel that bra would hold something from me like that.

Now tell me how am I suppose to have trust in woman that I feel lies to me about nothing? But blame it on what you feel, I'm just not ready to let go of this green eyed bandit.

So after all the whining, I told her the only way that I felt comfortable with the move is if she kept her apartment in Savannah. Reason being, is when she realizes that we're not going to work out, she won't feel so obligated to just hang around knowing she still has her own crib.

Like I told her, I'm really gonna miss that adventure part of our relationship, because I was more enthused in the with the fact that she was in a different city. To me, it really made spending time with her more intimate. You would have thought that she caught the drift, but, that's Teresa for you.

She say that she's gonna holler at her supervisor and see about her transferring. I just hope that she has enough sense to leave her transfer papers open for renegotiation.

"So playboy," I hear Slanga saying to me,

"are you ready to take the city by storm?"

I just looked over at him with a smirk similar to the one he gave me earlier, before I stressed, "What's understood, doesn't need to be talked about!"

(CHAPTER 4)

-KRUGER-

It's been two weeks since me and Slanga left Savannah. We both agreed to keep Firebug and that business to ourselves, so we really been on the grind hard.

This is my third shower since then. To me the hardest part of hustling is leaving the trap when you know that money is rolling through like fast food. The only reason I'm off now, is I need more work and Slanga about out too. He say we riding out later to get at Firebug, who's really been in our ear about reeing-up. Like I told Slanga, Firebug won't be tripping after he realizes how much we done hustled up.

Hell, I'm working with a little over 18 stacks and Slanga say he working with like 25. He also said that Firebug dropped the prices for us, cause he was taxing him like 2,800 for the big eighth. So the way I look at it, I'm gonna get it how I live while he's in such a good mood. If I can only get him to throw me a brick for this 18, I can make shit happen.

Me and Slanga would've left for the Sea-Port earlier, but I messed around and promised

Surina that I'll meet up with her later. Yeah, I said Surina.

She's been calling me dam near every day talking about she needs to holler at me, and she's just gonna keep calling until I see her. Leave it to my sister to give her my number. I got her picking me up from the Summer, so hopefully I can successfully close that chapter in a playa's life tonight.

What I really hate about this whole ordeal is the fact that I feel I'm breaking a promise to Deidra, and with that said, I'm realizing just how much I've grown to care for baby-girl. Life is really crazy like that.

Deidra has been that person that I've been able to rely on to do odds and ends for me without hesitation. She's really striving to get in where she fits in, and a playa can't help but respect the way that she's going about doing that.

I mean, just ask any genuine cat, and I say genuine because I feel that anybody can claim real. And who am I to differ? But every muthafucka can't say that they genuine, and a playa go for it. A genuine cat doesn't really have to say anything, you can actually see the sun shining off his forehead, but that's some other shit. The bottom line is I'm striving to only deal with genuine dudes these days.

Dam, with all that said, I can't understand how and why do I choose to deal with Teresa, and why in the hell did I just agree to see Surina?!

****

Surina nervously stood in front of her mirror appraising the outfit she wore. She had already tried on four different outfits, which were now scattered across her bed as her grandmother barged in her room.

"Girl, where you about to go?" Her grandmother asked after seeing all the clothes sprawled over the bed.

Surina was now agitated because her grandmother was now making a habit of just barging in her room, so she felt that she wasn't getting the privacy she deserved. But she knew better than to say anything about it, because she would've been reminded of how she never paid any bills.

"I gotta go and help Deidra put a perm in her hair," was her reply.

Her grandmother just shook her head before asking, "Did you know that boy Jimmy has been calling you all day?"

"If he calls back, just tell him that I'm sleep," was her response as she pinned up her hair.

"Girl, you know that I ain't with that lying!" Her grandmother stressed with aggression before adding, "Now if you don't wanna talk to that boy, be woman enough to let him know!"

"Yes mamm," Surina replied in a childlike manner before her grandmother walked out of the room.

Surina was relieved to see her walk away because she had enough on her mind already. She had just talked to Kruger and he'd told her to pick him up off Summer Street, so she was contemplating on what she was going to say to him. She felt that if she only said the right things, she had a good chance of getting him back.

The clock read 8:18 when she pulled in front of 1122 Summer Street. The house looked cold and dark as she witness zombie like people walking back and forth on the porch. After she blew the horn, Kruger emerged from one of the dark corners of the porch.

"So, where we going?" Was the first thing he asked after he got in the passenger seat.

"T.G.I. Fridays," she responded with a graceful smile before adding, "unless you had someplace else in mind."

Through the smile she wore, she was trying to ask his forgiveness for not doing right by him. In her mind, she felt that it wasn't time for the smile that said she'll do anything in the world to get him back.

"Na'll, I'm cool with that," is how he replied while adjusted his seat and adding, "I wish you would've got your man to cope you a bigger ride."

"Don't get in here making fun of the Civic," she stated in an attempt to break the friction between them before she added, "and for the record he ain't my man, you still are."

"Man, let's get this clear right now!" Is what he stated with a devious expression, "I don't know what your intentions are, but I want this over with as quickly as possible. See you violated our relationship, so you being my woman is totally out of the question!"

A lump appeared in her throat from his remark, but she knew she couldn't allow his rudeness to take her off her mission, so she stressed, "You should never say things like that to a woman who loves you unconditionally."

"Unconditionally love?" He questioned with a sly grin before adding, "You of all people couldn't possibly know the meaning of those words."

Surina could see all of her goals getting thrown out the window, so she took another approach and suggested, "Deamon, we only have a few hours together, so let's at least try to make the best of it."

He glared at her and she could tell that he wanted to say something harsh, so she gave him a smile that expressed the fact that she would rather make love to him all night, than anything else in the world.

Obviously he caught her vibe because he replied with, "Alright, I'm cool with that, but where is this gift you should've sent me two years ago?"

His sudden calmness gave her the impression that her make love smile worked every time, "I'll give it to you before we depart, just be patient," she assured him before giggling and asking, "do you remember how you use to tell me that?"

"I remember saying a lot of shit!" He retorted as she pulled in the restaurant's parking-lot, "But, it trips me out how you tend to remember what you wanna remember. Do you remember I use to say death before dishonor!"

She parked right next to the entrance of the

restaurant, since it wasn't that full. She knew that she had to hurry up and get out the car because she felt as if his spirit was suffocating her. As they both got of the car he said something that really made her realize just how much she hurt him.

"You dishonored our relationship, so now even our friendship is dead."

His words froze her at her car door. Surina could do nothing but stare at him for a few seconds. It took her a moment to build up the courage to actually move from the car.

As she walked towards him she knew that she couldn't look at herself in the mirror anymore if she just let things ride like the way they were, so she finally looked him dead in his eye and practically demanded, "Just tell me that you don't still have feelings for me in some way!"

He gazed at her for a moment showing the same gold teeth that she had drove him to the dentist to get. She was really upset because she never realized until now, how she had turned from his woman to his adversary. She felt that she could always had Deamon because they vowed to never part.

In her eyes he'd left her. Yeah, she knew that she should've written back, but it was his fault he'd left in the first place.

She knew that he was about to say some sort of smart remark so before he could, she gave him that make love smile again and humbly asked, "Can we just enjoy the night together?"

If she wasn't so sure before about her infamous smile, she was more than confident now, because he gave her a smirk, opened the door and announced, "After you Ms. Lady."

The hostess led them to a table by the window and for starters Kruger ordered two Hennessey's on the rocks. He then ordered a broccoli soup, a steak and a stuffed potato, while Surina was content with a chicken finger basket.

They were halfway through their meal when she revealed, "I have something that I've been trying to give you since you been home, but you wouldn't give me the time or date until now."

"Now tell me what really makes you think that I want anything from you?" He asked with a sarcastic expression.

She ignored him and confessed, "Baby, I have like 250 grams of that stuff ya'll be selling."

"Where the hell did you get that from?" He asked with a blank expression.

"Where do you think?!" She retorted with a sly grin.

"Where is it now?"

"In my trunk, along with a scale and a gun," she revealed before pausing for a moment and adding, "Deamon, I did it for you. I did it to show you where my heart is really at. Now, I know I may sound as if I'm talking crazy, but I really do love you."

He just shook his head and gave her that devilish grin again before she continued, "Now, the reason I never wrote you was."

She paused for a moment and tried to swallow the lump that was in her throat. As she stared at him she noticed how he was more attentive. That's when she realized that he really wanted to know what excuse she had.

"Like I said," she continued after taking a sip of her ice tea, "the reason I never wrote is, I really hated you for leaving me out here by myself. You have to remember that I was only nineteen when you got locked up, so I really didn't know what to say to you. I just knew that I missed you every second of the day."

He gave her a look as if to say, yeah right, before he stressed, "You could've wrote and told me the same thing you just said to me right here."

He then took a deep breath and added, "See playgirl, LOVE wouldn't have left me in a cell by myself! I'm sitting there wasting stamp money on a person who never took in consideration what I was going through. If you ask me, the only person Surina ever LOVED, was Surina!"

"Deamon, I know that you hate me for not staying in touch with you, but I also know that you still have some sort of feelings inside for me, or you wouldn't even be here," she stressed before he looked away from her and out the window.

She knew that she was finally hitting a nerve so she added, "Now, you can take the gift that I have for you, and at least a friendship invitation, so we can at least speak when we see each other. Or you can walk out of here being mad at me for the rest of your life, and mad at yourself for allowing your pride to stand in the way of a free 250 grams.

Now, if I was you," she continued, "I'd take my gift, and kill the bad blood between us. Besides, what am I gonna do with it?"

-KRUGER-

I believe that Firebug was more proud of

how much we had brought to the table than he led us to believe. But his reaction was understandable, taking into consideration the situation he had going on with his three guys in Atlanta.

He hipped us to the fact that they got popped by the Feds, and he didn't really know where they stood on the code of silence. The only thing that he knew was that all three of them was already back on the street. To top it all off, they never called him and stress the fact that they even had a situation of the sort.

Now this is the part where Slanga feels it's time to earn stripes or whatever he wants to call himself up to. He ended up suggesting to Firebug, that me and him take care of the question marks. The reason he says that he made the suggestion was, if they called Firebug's name, our name was subject to come up somewhere down the line.

You know I feel where he coming from, but there's something that he might have neglected to look at. The only way that our names could come up is through Firebug. So that's like saying Firebug is a potential snitch too. But like I said, I feel where he coming from, eliminate the problem before it gets to that point.

So yeah, let's make it happen, cause it ain't

no way that I can see myself going back to prison behind a questioned mark that couldn't hold his weight.

They're from College Park, and are well known city wide tricks, so they stayed in and out of strip clubs. Their favorite club was Magic City, but every Wednesday night you could find them at Strokers. So their official last night on earth had to be Wednesday.

We left Savannah that Tuesday night in a black Lincoln Town, headed for Atlanta with a black bag full of accessories for the job. Firebug had hooked us up. In my bag was two 45's, Slanga had two Glock .40's. We both had black *Polo* jeans, t-shirts, jackets, socks, gloves, boots and a mask. It made me wonder if we was doing a hit for the old man or Ralph Lauren.

Amanda and Firebug's twins, Stacy and Tracy, was in a black Cadillac leading the way. We ended up staying at the Hilton in the two rooms Firebug had reserved for us. I shared a room with the twins, while Slanga spent some quality time with Amanda.

Stacy and Tracy wasn't identical, but they were both sexy in their own way. Stacy was the oldest by four minutes. I knew this because everytime they would argue, she'd bring it up and Tracy would say, "what's four minutes?" Besides being the oldest, she was also the shortest and thickest. Stacy had a body similar to Ki'Toy, while Tracy was taller and built more like those twins off that show Sister-Sister.

Firebug gave me the green light to do whatever I pleased with them, but I was content with everybody just knowing their positions for the following night.

Our targets pulled in *Strokers* parking-lot a quarter after eleven in a burgundy Navigator. As soon as they stepped out their truck, the girls were walking towards the door. Now me and Slanga are in a position to see everything, so that we could pick the best opportunity to make our move.

We watched Stacy's thick ass dropped her purse just as them cats walked up towards them by the door. The biggest of the three looked her up and down before he obviously felt that she was worth him bending over and picking it up for her. Being that she had on a mini skirt that never seemed to make it fully over her ass, buddy was caught up.

I saw her giggle as buddy looked up at her with a wide grin. After taking a peek and realizing that she wasn't wearing any panties, he went to another galaxy. The next thing I knew they all were getting back in their rides and pulling off, with the girls leading the way.

Ten minutes later we all was pulling into this gas station. Me and Slanga parked on the side of the store and stepped out, strapped up. When we stepped around the front, one of the cats was coming out the store with a case of beer. With no hesitation, he caught two slugs to the chest and one to the head.

The one who had picked up Stacy's purse, was pumping the gas, so he caught a slug to the chest and two to the head. When I walked up to him, he was in a state of shock, obviously from seeing his partner getting gun down. Tears was flowing down his cheeks but he wasn't whimpering or nothing. The last cat died on the toilet in the unisex bathroom inside the store. Slanga had put seven holes in him.

The getaway was as smooth as one could have predicted. I jumped in the Lincoln with the twins and Slanga jumped in the Caddy with Amanda, so the girls drove us back to Savannah.

I was more comfortable on the way back then I was on the drive there. We was halfway to Savannah when I thought about how I could have blew us all up if I would've hit one of those pumps. The little jitters I did had was flushed away by the twins making jokes.

They was tripping about how that one dude eyes looked when Slanga opened the door with them two huge pistols. Those crazy broads couldn't stop laughing and talking about how they never wanted to die on the toilet.

-TERESA-

I don't know what has been going on with Deamon lately, but he's really pissed me off this time. I can't believe that he had the nerve to tell me that he's going to get Ron to help me move. I wanted to tell his ass that Ron ain't my dam man, but as usual, I just let it ride.

Right now him and Slanga is in Orlando. Now I know that his job ain't paying enough for him to be vacationing in Orlando. His ass has to be back selling drugs, because he's coming up with all sorts of things that I know he can't afford on his salary.

Ron won't tell me nothing and Toya claims that she don't know nothing. Her ass has been staying in Augusta for over a week and she still claims that she don't know nothing!

I'm supposed to be starting work at the Medical prison in Augusta in a couple of weeks. I've made arrangements to move in with Toya until I can find something that I feel is worth having. I'm definitely not about to move to another city just to stay in their slums. Hell, I can just stay here for that. So that's definitely out of the question.

For some awkward reason or the other, my ex, David has been writing me lately. It's funny because he stop writing me months ago. I thought maybe he got the hint when I never responded to any of the letters. I told Deamon about it and he says that David probably just needs some money.

Deamon then reaches into his pocket, pulls out four hundred dollar bills and tells me to make sure I send that to David. I asked him why, and all he did was kiss me on my forehead and told me to just take care of it.

Now he has to know that he has really confused me with this one. Usually, a man hates the fact that his woman is keeping some sort of communication cord with her ex, but with him giving me money to send mine, he's only encouraging it. I never heard of something like this going down before, so I really don't know how to take him.

Last night I told him that I wanted to have his baby. Hell, I even told the man that I've been trying to get pregnant. He said that he figured as much after I kept trying to lock his legs so that he couldn't pull out.

I don't know what this dude be thinking about at times, because he never expresses himself, at least not to me anyway. It's like he's holding so much inside, but I don't know what to do to make him vent. I try to get him to talk to me, but I'm better off talking to the walls. I mean, am I so wrong to want my man to talk to me?

-KRUGER-

To be honest, I'm kind of cool with the position I found myself in this morning. Here it is the middle of July and me Slanga, Amanda and Deidra down here lounging in Orlando. Firebug and them crazy twins were suppose to fly down, but I guess they had other plans. When I really think about it, all of us needed a vacation after these past few weeks.

I really didn't wanna bring Deidra at first,

but now I'm glad I did. If I would've brought Teresa, her ass would've been in my ear nagging me about this or that. You know, just a lot of shit that really don't concern her. Besides, to keep it genuine I feel that I was neglecting Deidra a little bit anyway.

I mean, me and Slanga have stayed in Savannah for over a week on account of the hit we had to pull, so Teresa was seeing me more often. Which really isn't fair to Deidra, because she's been putting in a lot more work than Teresa.

You know what really kills me with Teresa is the fact that I know she's still wondering why I gave her money to send that dude David. Even after we've had the discussion about Surina and the way I feel that she had left me for dead. But maybe one day she'll finally recognize that I was just in that same position.

I knew that ole boy just needed money, because why else would he put his pride to the side after all this time to get back in touch with her. He had to be really ass out to write after a year. But like I said, maybe one day she'll understand.

Every since we did that hit everything been running smooth for a playa. Firebug showed us major love. He hit us off with ten stacks and a half a brick a piece. I ended up giving Burger a quarter for four and a half stacks back. When I get back, my goal is to eventually do that for all my homies. I wish that I could show them all that love at one time, but I ain't built like that just yet.

I still have that quarter brick Surina gave me. Sometimes I feel that I shouldn't have taken it, but then I be like dam that, it was FREE.

The other day I snatched all my dope out of the trunk of my Caddy and let Deidra put it up in her Daddy's house. I had to do something with it, because I didn't wanna mess around and fall victim like that cat Jimmy did. Besides, who's really gonna go searching for dope at the police house, a Christian police at that. Now with that part of the game secured, I can really focus on getting this money.

"Deamon," I hear Deidra calling my name after she walked in the room.

She has to know that I'm still on this balcony gazing at the sky.

"Deamon," is what she practically chanted in this seductive manner as she blocked the sun from shinning on my face.

She has on this pink and brown DKNY two piece bathing suit that has her looking good enough to chew on right now.

134

"What up baby-girl?" I replied as I sat up.

"Slanga say you need to come on down to the pool and get out of this room," she informed me.

"He got his phone with him?"

"I think so," she answered as she walked back into the room.

I'm only a step behind her. Man, I swear this girl is getting thicker or something. The way this ass is maneuvering in front of me has my mind on something else right now, so I grabbed my phone and called Slanga.

"Yeah," he answered after the third ring.

"What up?" I asked as I heard people in the background playing in the pool.

"Man, bring your ass down here so that you can jump in this pool!"

I looked over at Deidra sashaying throughout the room and told him, "Man, I'm gonna have to hit that pool up a little later, cause I see something else I wanna jump in right now."

After hearing what I said she walked towards me.

"Well, handle your business playboy, just

get at me later," is what I heard Slanga say before I pushed the end button on my phone.

"So you were looking to get inside of me?" She questioned in a seductive manner as she grabbed the phone out of my hand and placed it on the end table.

"Now what makes you think that?" I sarcastically cross-examined.

"And what makes you think that I feel like playing the guessing game with you?" Is how she responded as she took a step back before taking off her bathing suit.

Now watching her do this little strip tease had me open. At that moment I realized how foolish I was back in the day for choosing Surina over her.

Forty-five minutes later we were in the shower. Now that I really think about it, she's really the only female that I don't have some type of grudge against. I guess that's why it's so easy for her to turn me on the way she do.

From the moment she showed up at my mama's house with that bottle, I've been questioning her motive. So naturally I throw all type of test at her, but she passes them all with flying colors. There's no doubt in my mind that she knows and plays her position well. Now tell me how can a playa continue to neglect someone like that?

****

"What do you mean Weasy?" Jimmy was asking as he drove to Tom-Tom's house.

"Just like I said big homie," he replied as he rolled a blunt, "I know that you have mad feelings for ole girl, but you have to know that you can't trust her like you think."

"It sounds to me as if you know something that I don't," Jimmy implied with a look of concern.

"Listen playboy, the broad just ain't no good," Weasel revealed as he licked the blunt shut.

He then looked over at Jimmy and added, "You know I wouldn't be surprised if she the one that hit us up for that pack."

"Look Weasy, you gotta feel me on this one," Jimmy insisted, "because this is the first time that I'm ever hearing anything negative about Surina."

"Well, check this out. I have this broad who

works at T.G.I. Fridays and she say that she seen Surina in there with a dark skin cat with gold teeth, and she ended up paying for the meal," he finally revealed before lighting the blunt and adding, "Now the only nigga I feel that she'll do that for is Kruger."

"I knew that nigga was gonna be a problem!" Jimmy spat out.

Weasel just looked over at him with a look of disgust before shaking his head.

"Now what?" Jimmy stressed after seeing him shake his head.

"See, that's why I didn't wanna tell your ass shit, because you don't know how to handle the situation."

Jimmy looked over at him with a confused expression.

"I mean, do you actually hear yourself?" Weasel questioned him before pausing for a moment and adding, "Playboy, you're breaking the number one rule in the game, NEVER CHECK THE PIMP, CHECK THE HOE!

I told your ass before, that ole boy don't chase them broads, he let them come to him, and this here is the main reason why!" Weasel continued, "See, when you let them come to you, that gives you more leverage and you can detect their motives quicker than you can going to them. You know it's some real scandalous broads out here, some more openly than others."

Jimmy now wore a dumbfounded expression as he watched the road.

After taking another pull from the blunt, Weasel passed it to Jimmy and added, "The real question you need to be asking is, what did they have to talk about, cause they ain't fucking."

"How you know they ain't fucking?"

"Cause nigga, I'm real! And real recognize real!" He revealed with a sly grin.

Jimmy obviously never caught the notion that at the moment Weasel didn't considered him real.

"Now let me ask you this," Weasel continued, "if you got locked-up and your lady didn't write or even had the common respect to acknowledge that she knew you was still alive, would you get out and fuck with her as if she ain't did shit wrong?"

"Man, I," Jimmy stuttered out before Weasel interrupted.

"Hold up, let me answer that for you, HELL NO! You can't go back to fucking with her like that, cause she gonna feel that it's alright to fuck you over whenever she thinks it's appropriate. She feels that she can violate whenever, because all she has to do is give you the pussy to make amends. So to never find yourself in that position, you never go backwards, just stay focused on what's in front of you."

Jimmy allowed what he was just told marinate for a moment before he stressed, "You know to be a young nigga, you got a helluva way of thinking."

"And guess what, the nigga who really put me on point is even younger than me."

"Kruger?"

"Yeah fool, Kruger," Weasel assured him as Jimmy pulled in Tom-Tom's driveway, "that's how I know that he ain't fucking her, cause that'll go against everything he stands for. And if you don't stand for something, you're bound to fall for anything."

Tom-Tom was sitting on the porch watching his two man team discuss an obvious touchy subject as they sat in the car for a moment. He was a short and round older cat who people often said reminded them of the guy who starred in that sitcom Roc.

"Dam younguns, what's with the long face?" Is what he asked after they got out the car.

"It ain't nothing old man, we just sad at the fact that you haven't lost any weight yet," Weasel stressed as he embraced him.

Tom-Tom just chuckled before, "I'm content with this here, but if you keep smoking them big ass blunts you're gonna be twice my size."

"Yeah right, I'm straight just like I am. I mean, I ain't slim or round, I'm in between," Weasel revealed as he took a seat next to Tom-Tom.

"Yeah, in between meals," Jimmy stated causing all three of them to burst out laughing.

Thirty minutes later they were pulling off with their usual package.

"Say Weasel," Jimmy stated as he turned down the sounds of UGK's, 'Riding Dirty', "what do you suggest I should do about Surina?"

"I wouldn't do anything different but I also wouldn't put that much trust in her either."

"Do you really think that she could have got us for that pack?" Jimmy asked.

Weasel just looked over at him and shook his head again before sadly replying, "With you even asking me that, I know she could have. She's the perfect suspect, the one you least expect."

"But, what would she do with it?"

Weasel couldn't believe the simple questions he was asking, "See that's your problem right there. I know you see everything going down, but you have so many feelings and emotions involved that you're actually walking around here with a blindfold."

(CHAPTER 5)

It was one of those moments where all the fellas were on the porch of 1122, while Georgia Slim was getting his hair braided by Red's mama, Ms. Red.

Ms. Red was the female impression of her son. The only difference was the fact that she got high, but the fellas had made it a house rule to never sell to her. That was just a rule created out of respect of Red.

"Dam Ms. Red," Georgia Slim Stressed, "It's too tight!"

"Boy, stop acting like you all sensitive and shit!" She retorted.

"Mama, If you gonna do his hair, do it!" Red stressed with a cold stare.

"Stop tripping all the time boy, you never let your mama have no fun," she replied in a childlike manner.

"So, you know you ain't suppose to be over here anyway!" He stressed before adding, "I'm just trying to let you make a little money."

"I told ya'll that nigga thinks he my daddy," she revealed causing everybody on the porch to laugh.

"He only trying to look out for you," Pimp interjected.

"Mind your business, you one arm bitch!" She snapped with a gruesome expression.

Ms. Red just happened to be one of the few people who could talk to the fellas like that. The other was probably, the owner of the boarding house, Ms. Mildred.

"Say Kruger, you know that Ms. Mildred been looking for you," Rip stressed.

"Oh yeah," Kruger replied.

"Yeah, she says you owe her a hundred dollars."

"Man, I had done forgot all about that." Kruger confessed.

"Just give me the money, cause I already handled that," Rip revealed.

"I preciate that playboy," Kruger stressed as he reached in his pocket and pulled out a wad of bills, "here is 150, cause I know she was giving you hell."

"Nigga, if that's the case, you owe all of us some cheese, cause you know she was cursing everybody out!" Hamburger stressed.

"I hope none of ya'll ain't dirty," Big Ox calmly stated, "cause here come the narcs rolling thru."

They all were calm, as usual, under the circumstances. Lately the narcotic squad was riding thru Summer Street as if it was their home. The last time they stopped by, Kruger and Gunslanga was in Orlando and they ended up finding 4,300 on Rip.

Big Ox started up a conversation about a Donald Goines novel that they all seem to have read. So that was the topic of conversation when the four car caravan stopped in front of the boarding house.

There was a burgundy Lumina, a black Lumina, a blue Jimmy truck and a gold Explorer parked directly behind each other, with no less than three agents in each of them. After they all stepped out, Lt. Honeycutt was the first to speak.

"Ya'll have a helluva regime here," he stated with a cold stare.

"From the looks of it, you working with a little something yourself," Hamburger replied.

Honeycutt was a tall lanky middle aged white man who was on his ninth year on the squad. During that period, he'd seen his share of corruption on both sides of his shield. He started from the bottom and now all moves within the squad were directed under his supervision.

"I know that ya'll boys don't mind if I get me a little photo of this regime?" The lieutenant asked with a sly grin.

"We got your muthafuckin boys!" Georgia Slim retorted, "And, hell na'll! Unless you gonna leave us with a photo of ya'll."

"Now why would you want a photo of us?" Honeycutt asked with a sly grin.

"The same reason you want one of us," Rip replied.

"And how much money do you have on you today, Mr. Strong?" He asked Rip with a sly grin.

"This must be one of those police harassment situations," Kruger stressed with a smirk.

"I wouldn't say that Mr. Pearsey, and might I add that it's good to see that you and Mr. Frazier has made it back home in one piece," he stated as he looked over at Kruger and Gunslanga, "how was

146

your trip up the road anyway?"

"Everything was all good on our end," Gunslanga assured, "we had the same family support you see right here. But for future references, I think you need to watch how you always voice your opinion on people's lives."

Gunslanga wore a devilish grin that seem to only make the red headed Honeycutt's face attempt to get redder than his hair.

"Let's cut the chase boys!" He practically demanded before Red cut him off.

"The only boys I know is white boys and cowboys, and it looks to me as if you fit both descriptions."

"Whatever, but what we came for is your photos, not your opinions!" He responded openly aggravated.

"Now tell me, what we look like making shit sweet for you?" Georgia Slim implied before adding, "The only way you can get pictures of us is if we can get pictures of you."

"You know that you're a little too small to be running your mouth like that!" Honeycutt stressed with a sinister grin.

"Ain't nobody gonna fuck with him, so he

can say what he feels!" Kruger stated with no regret, "See, what you fail to realize is, that badge ya'll got don't scare nobody out here. You bleed just like we do! Just like we got family, you got family. Just like you're looking to snatch us from our family, you can look for us to do the same!"

Honeycutt just smiled before replying with, "Mr. Pearsey, you're in violation of your parole by sitting on this porch selling crack."

"Now why would you play yourself like that? You know, just like I know, that if I was in any kind of violation, you'll be the first one dragging me down to 401," he replied with a sly grin.

"It was nice seeing you officers today," Hamburger stressed, "but right now I think you have worn out your welcomes."

"Man, you can't make us take a picture because we sitting on a porch that we pay rent at!" Georgia Slim stressed, "If that was the case, you'll have pictures of dam near everybody in Augusta."

"We tried to make a trade with you, but since you refused, we'll holler," Black stated.

Honeycutt was furious, but he ordered his agents to their cars.

"Say Martin," Pimp called out to one of the

agents, "tell ole girl you lay next to on Kissingbower Road that I won't be able to make it to dinner tonight."

Agent Martin had always harassed Pimp whenever he saw him, but at the time he could only stare at him in shock.

"Yeah, I thought that you might feel that way," he added after seeing the expression on his face, "you'd be surprised about what we know."

****

"Bitch, you think I don't know that you're fucking Deamon!" Surina practically yelled at Deidra.

They were sitting across from each other in Red Lobster. They had already been to the mall, and a few other department stores until they decided to eat at Red Lobster. The day seemed to be a usual for them, until Deidra made a comment about Surina and Deidra.

"Girl, calm down, I know you know!" Deidra replied openly embarrassed.

"Then tell me why you're fucking my man!"

149

STUCK

Surina demanded to know.

Deidra looked around the semi crowded restaurant and realizes that everyone was focused on their table so she attempted to ease the situation, "Let's just let it go."

"That's exactly what your ass should've done, let it go! How you get to be fucking my man anyway, bitch?!" Surina stressed.

"First of all, he ain't your man!" Deidra strongly stated in a whisper, "Hell, he ain't even mine! And don't act as if you don't know that he don't want nothing else to do with you."

"So that gave you the right to go and fuck him cause you felt that I couldn't?!"

"Look Surina, I know I was wrong in a sense, but once it went down the first time I couldn't just stop seeing him," she replied as she gazed down at the table.

"Bitch, it should have never been a first time!" She snapped back before taking a deep breath and adding, "You know what really kills me is the fact that you act as if you haven't done anything wrong. I mean, you still call me, we still go out and everything."

"Oh, we were suppose to stop being friends

because who I'm having sex with?" She asked in illusion.

After Surina didn't answer Deidra added, "If you feel like that, then we were never friends to begin with."

"Deidra, you're fucking my ex, now that's something I could never do to you!" She pointed out with tears flowing down her cheeks.

Deidra sat there for a moment and thought about how Surina was feeling, but she also thought about how she felt. The way she was looking at it, she had put her feelings to the side for Surina long enough for one lifetime. She was now prepared to do something for herself, instead of always doing for Surina.

"Well, if you take me home, we don't never have to worry about being friends again," Deidra finally replied with no signs of remorse.

"I'm through with it, and your trifling ass can walk home, bitch!" Surina rose from her seat and stormed out the restaurant.

Deidra sat there for a moment before she grabbed her phone and called Deamon.

"Speak," he stated after the second ring.

"Deamon," she called out.

"Yeah, what's happening baby-girl?"

"I'm stranded at Red Lobster and I need a ride."

"Where your car at?"

"At home," she replied before taking a deep breath and adding, "I was riding with Surina and we fell out, so she left me here."

"You ate yet?"

"No, we just got here."

"Well, order me a steak and lobster, with an extra lobster tail, and I'll be there in the next ten minutes."

"Alright baby," she managed to get out before the line went dead.

The waitress walked over and asked if everything was alright. She just nodded her head and ordered their food. After the waitress left she sat there baffled as she pondered over her next move.

The way she was looking at it, she felt Kruger was going to be angry about everything. He had already told her to be careful around Surina. So in her eyes he had every right to be upset.

The one thing that she loved and respected

about Kruger was the fact that he never tried to tell her to leave Surina alone. The way she took it was that he respected her enough not to put her in a position of choosing between them.

Deidra knew that it wasn't going to be long before Surina would find out and eventually do what she had just did. She was really relieved that the incident didn't escalate to something bigger. One side of her felt that she was in the wrong, but the other side continued to tell her to live for herself. She didn't want to be selfish, but she was finally happy.

To her, Kruger had all of the qualities she preferred in a man. He was loving, in his own way. Not to mention how sexy, considerate and loyal he was. No one knew that he was the main reason she really never had a boyfriend. She would always compare everybody she met to him, and to her, none never measured up. He was always like that prized mate, so when the opportunity came, she took advantage of it.

She knew all about Teresa, so she felt that she was the one woman who knew more than any. The way Teresa looked at it, Deidra was one of Kruger's clients. She never realized that whenever he wasn't with her or on Summer Street, he was cuddled up somewhere with Deidra.

"Dam, baby-girl, is everything alright with you?" Kruger snuck up and asked her.

She looked up to see him standing over her. He then bent over and kissed her on the forehead, before he took a seat across from her.

"So what happened?" He asked.

"She just blurted out that you're still her man and I shouldn't be kicking it with you," she replied with a pessimistic expression.

"Are you alright, or do you need to stay the night with me?" He asked with a sly grin.

She grinned back and replied with, "I need to stay with you."

"That's cool. You know that I can take care of you tonight, but you have to promise that you're gonna get up in the morning with a smile."

She blushed before her face turned serious and she asked, "Can you tell me why you still kick it with me?"

The shocked expression he now wore let her know that she caught him off guard.

"Why you ask?" He questioned.

"I guess because I tend to ask myself the same question. At first I knew you messed with me to get back at her, but that was months ago," she stressed before pausing and seeing his nonchalant expression before she added, "Now, I wanna know why you still kicking it with me?"

He couldn't help but smile before he replied with, "First of all, have you seen yourself in the mirror lately?" This caused her to blush so he added, "Yeah, you tight like that. But the real reason I kick it with you is, you never try to be someone or something you're not. So far, you have been what I call genuine, and with me that gets you farther than a big butt and a phony smile."

"Did you know that I'm in love with you?" She asked him in a sincere manner.

It took him a moment to respond with, "Believe it or not, you just happen to be the only female I ever been with who's actions always spoke louder than her words. So yeah, I knew it way before you even had the nerve to say it," he replied with a genuine smile.

She then rose from her seat and asked, "Do you think that we can get our food to go?"

"Yeah, we can do that," he agreed as he stood up.

"Deamon," she said his name in a soft whisper.

"Yeah, what up boo?"

"I thought that you should be the first to know that I'm pregnant," she stated as she walked up to him and looked into his eyes.

She had found out the day before, but she had told herself that she wasn't going to tell him right away. But after the conversation they just had, she thought that it would be best to let him know now. But as she gazed into his confused eyes, she was now wondering if she'd made the right decision.

"Baby, you ain't mad are you?" She asked with a look of concern.

"Now why would I be mad at you, what you do so wrong?" He replied.

"So do you want me to have the baby?"

A smirk appeared on his face before he replied with, "The question is, do you want to have the baby?"

"You already know I do!" She spat out, "I just know how you and Teresa have ya'll thing going and I have to respect that, because that was going down before I threw myself in the middle. I just wanted to be just as considerate as you are before I decided to make my decision."

"I can feel you on that, but I'm all for it. The thing is, I just want us to keep this on the low until we find a way to bring it to the light, you cool with that?"

"Of course boo, I'm definitely cool with that!" She stated as she hugged him.

****

Firebug sat in the living room of his five bedroom home on the south-side of Savannah with his old protégé, Big Wade. It was Tuesday afternoon and they were watching The Young and The Restless on his sixty inch screen. If you knew Firebug, you knew that at this time of the day, he was not to be bothered.

As far as Big Wade was concerned, he was considered the backbone of the organization. With him, everything was handled by the codes of the streets, every violation had an appropriate consequence.

Big Wade would always tell Firebug, "If you let them get away with a gram, they'll eventually be back for a kilo!"

Before Big Wade met up with Firebug he

was known on the streets of Savannah for shooting at will. He was already doing a little hustling of his own but he was lacking two of the most important qualities of a successful hustler, discipline and a good connect. Firebug eventually put him under his wing, and they soon became known, in Savannah, as the man and the machine.

While Firebug was in prison, Big Wade was the one who was in charge, and he successfully kept everything in order. He knew of everyone they dealt with except for Gunslanga and Kruger.

He had heard plenty from Firebug, who practically praised the youngsters. True enough they were making more money than expected, but Big Wade knew from experience that anyone could make money. To most hustlers making money was the easy part, what most struggled with was finding a way to invest and keep it.

Big Wade had seen so many come and go and often referred to them as, minute men. To earn his respect, you had to have longevity. To him, without that, you was just another squirrel trying to get a nut.

The only flaw that Big Wade visually had was his high expense account towards his female companions. But he would always tell Firebug, "It ain't tricking if you got it!"

"Say Firebug," Big Wade stressed, "What time are we suppose to meet up with your two younguns?"

"I told them to meet us at Longhorns at two, so they'll be walking through the door at 1:55," Firebug stipulated with a wide grin.

At 2:02 Big Wade and Firebug were walking through the restaurant doors, while Gunslanga and Kruger sat at the table in the back. If this was a night club, the section that they sat in would be considered as VIP.

When Kruger saw them approaching, he tapped his comrade and they both stood up to greet them.

"What's going Firebug?" Kruger stressed.

"Same ole shit, just a different day," he replied with a light smile before adding, "say fellas, I asked ya'll to come here so ya'll both can meet Big Wade."

Everyone greeted and embraced each other before Firebug spoke again, "Me and Wade has been handling business together for over ten years, so I can honestly say that I trust this man with my life. He's one of the few cats that always know where I am, so he knows about every transaction we've made. I said all that just to let ya'll know where he stands in my eyes."

After everyone took a seat, Big Wade said, "The old man speaks highly of you two. He talks about ya'll more than he use to talk about his nephew Lil Rick, and he had half of the Sea- Port on lock in the early 90's," he stated causing them both to smile, "that's the real reason I'm here. I couldn't pass up the opportunity to meet the two who has captured the attention of the old man the way you have."

"I probably heard just as much about you too, so the feeling is mutual," Gunslanga replied.

"Yeah, Big Wade, as you just heard, Firebug speaks highly of you too," Kruger pointed out as he looked over at Gunslanga before adding, "we both have a lot of love and respect for him, so we respect his opinion of you."

A sly grin appeared on Big Wade's face as if he had just found what he'd been looking for, "One thing I want ya'll to remember, so you won't be disappointed in either of us, and you might be blessed to live a little longer." He urged, "Never settle for what another man says about anyone, always grasp your own opinion.

160

If a cat looks suspicious when you first meet him," he continued, "keep your guard up, and don't let it down until he's dead and gone. See me and the old man are still human, so we do make mistakes."

Gunslanga and Kruger just nodded their heads to let him know that they understood.

"Life is too short to really trust anybody," Big Wade added, "my own mama hit me for sixteen grand. It wasn't about the money, it was how she got it. It's never the situation, always the principle."

"I assure you that we both can feel where you're coming from on that," Gunslanga stressed as he looked over at Kruger.

Firebug just smiled at the way that his newest protégés handled Big Wade's interrogation before he got to the main business at hand, "So what ya'll looking to spend?"

"We want the same four we got last time," Gunslanga revealed.

"Look, don't start that falling off shit!" Firebug blasted, "Ya'll already know that ya'll done spoiled me. I'm use to ya'll copping a bigger package every trip, so let this be the last time with this petty hustling."

"No problem Pop, we just had to close shop cause them folks kept riding through harassing lately," Kruger announced.

"Do you know the agents name?" Big Wade asked.

"Yeah," Kruger replied, "the head man name is Honeycutt."

"Do you think that ya'll need some help up there?" Firebug asked.

"Not really, cause we working with enough cats to handle any situation," Gunslanga assured before adding, "the problem is, we don't know where most of them rest their head."

"Well, we can work on getting that information for you, but do ya'll really feel you can work it from there?" Firebug insisted to know.

"If you can get that, we can easily take care of the problem," Kruger assured.

"Listen," Big Wade stated, "we are gonna get that information for you, but eliminating them is only gonna bring more heat and more agents who you know less about. So when we do get this info., it's best you try to pay these cats off." He stated before he exposed a gruesome grin on his face before he added, "Now if they don't

162

cooperate after that, then like Keisha said on New Jack City, rock-a-bye-baby!"

As usual, they finished conducting their business before they all departed. They each wore smiles that said they were more confident in their future then when they walked in the restaurant.

****

Lieutenant Honeycutt stood in front of his fourteen or so agents inside of the narcotics division of the Augusta precinct as he discussed their previous operations.

In the last three months they had arrested ninety-four dealers from tips from confidential informants. But just two days ago, four of those informants were found dead in a abandon warehouse. Each of them were laying side by side hog-tied with their tongues in their pockets.

"Now gentlemen, we must assist homicide in some way to find a lead in this case." He instructed as he paced back and forth, "Now, if we can't help keep our informants safe, then they'll be too frightened to help us in the future. Without them, that would only put us back on the street,

163

starting at the bottom again. So as much as I hate to ask you, I still have to do my job. Do any of you have some sort of lead to where this leak came from?"

Neither of his agents responded as they sat erect in their seats.

Honeycutt just shook his head after seeing the dumbfounded expression on each of their faces and added, "Somebody is moving some major weight in our city and they refuse for us to get, even an inch close. Now, I know most of you have family to tend to, but in order to get to the bottom of this epidemic, we have to start taking double shifts. If this situation goes further than it has, we won't have a city to live in."

****

Deidra sat on her living room couch waiting on her father, who had called her a few hours earlier saying that he had to talk to her.

The moment she hung up with him, she moved Kruger's package from her room to the shed in the backyard, because she didn't know whether he had stumbled on it or not. All she knew was she wasn't in the position to be taking any chances.

What bothered her more than anything was the fact that she wasn't accustomed to her father leaving her in suspense like this. So when he finally pulled into the driveway, she ran outside to greet him.

"What's wrong daddy?" She asked with a genuine look of concern.

"Nothing really Dee," he replied as he stepped out his car, "I just want you to be more cautious on who you choose as friends."

"So what's going on, what are you talking about?"

"We had a multiple homicide the other night and for some reason your friend Deamon's name came up." He replied before looking down at his daughter and seeing her dumbfounded expression, "Now there is no evidence pointing towards him, it's just a lot of hearsay coming from the narcotics division, but I wanted you to be on point, just in case I have to bring him in for questioning."

"Why would you have to bring him in, if there is no evidence against him?"

"Because his name keeps coming up." He replied before adding, "Look, the only reason I'm letting you know is, I know that you really care for him."

"Thank you daddy," she replied as they walked through the front door.

She hugged her father before she walked in her room and closed the door. She then grabbed her phone as she laid on her bed. Her first thought was to call Deamon, but she just laid there and stared at the ceiling for a moment instead.

The news didn't hit her as hard as her father thought it did, because Kruger had already told her to be on the lookout for the conversation. She could tell that her father really was curious about whether or not she knew anything about the homicides.

For times like this she wished that her mother was still alive, because she knew how uncomfortable her and her father's conversation usually were. She really wanted to assure him that she was alright, but she couldn't' think of a way, so she dialed Kruger's number.

"What up baby-girl?" He asked after answering.

"He say that your name keeps coming up in

166

those murders, so he might have to bring you in for questioning," she replied.

"I know that it may sound bad, but like I told you, everything is all good. Just let your daddy know that'll I'll meet up with him, but only at ya'll house."

"Alright, but don't you think he needs to know that I'm carrying your baby?" She suggested.

"I don't know if that's a good idea, because he'll probably think that I put you up to tell him that. So he'll start thinking that I'm in the wrong somewhere," he explained.

"I can understand that, but you have to know that I still want him to know," she implied.

"And you have to know that I'm cool with all of that, but I wanna be there with you to tell him. That way he'll know that you didn't get pregnant by no busta."

"I love you, so please be careful out there."

"Don't worry boo, I ain't going nowhere," he stressed, "it's gonna take more than just a bunch of washed up detectives to keep me from my first born."

"So, am I gonna see you tonight?"

"Just get the room and call and let me know

where you at," he replied.

"You know I love you right?" She practically declared.

"What's understood doesn't need to be talked about!"

(CHAPTER 6)

Danny Singleton sat behind his desk watching parolees enter and exit. It was the first Monday in August and all of his parolees were schedule to report. Singleton was a middle aged gambler with a debt as deep as his future grave.

He was busy typing something in his computer when the front desk called.

"Mr. Singleton, there is a Deamon Pearsey here to see you."

"Send him in, please."

A few seconds later Kruger entered his office.

"Good morning, Mr. Singleton," he greeted while stepping in and closing the door behind him.

"How are you doing Pearsey, do you have your supervision fee?" He replied without taking his eyes away from his computer.

"Yeah, I got that," Kruger responded as he took a seat.

"Now, brief me on all this racket I hear

about you and Frazier being connected to those people found dead in that warehouse?" He asked before finally looking at Kruger.

"Obviously they're just rumors since I'm not in 401 charged with anything," Kruger replied with a sly grin.

"Might I remind you, Mr. Pearsey, that you have a little over four years remaining on your parole, so I advise you not do anything stupid to get sent back." He stated in a professional manner before adding, "See, out here you can become somebody special, but in there you're just another number, and with another smart remark like that, you might just find yourself right back where you started."

Without uttering a word, Kruger rose from his seat and dug in his pocket. He pulled out a money order and five hundred dollar bills before placing them on Singleton's desk.

"What is this?" Singleton asked while picking up the money.

"That's five hundred to help pay that gambling debt you have with the bookie Dead-Eyedown at Robbie's on Washington Road." He stressed as he watched Singleton's face go from powerful to powerless.

"See Mr. Singleton," Kruger continued, "all those intimidation tactics you were trained to enforce, won't get either of us anywhere. Now you can take the money and five more every report day, for you to continue to do what you've been doing or Mrs. Singleton can find out about Dead-Eye and twenty year old Belinda, who you've been creeping with for the last seven months."

"How do you know this, who told you these things?" He stuttered.

"I'll see you next month on report day, and make sure you get at Dead-Eye, cause he known to get stupid about his money at times," Kruger responded before walking out of Singleton's office.

-KRUGER-

Here I am inside a hotel suite with a fifth of *Hennessy* and an ounce of hydroponic to put my mind at ease. Hell, with the information I got on Singleton, I can smoke my back out and ain't gotta worry about a urine test.

Man, It's been like a week or so since they found them bodies, so the heat has been on the Summer real strong. At first we only had the narcs rolling through, but now we have homicide detectives stopping by more than the fiends.

Deidra's pop is the lead investigator on the case and I know he feels that I had something to do with it, but with no evidence or witnesses, you have no case. Besides, no-one is really concerned about those bodies but the law.

I know Deidra's pop don't want me dealing with her, but right now it is what it is. Just like any other father, he would rather have her with a doctor or lawyer type of cat, but he knows that she's more attracted to street cats. I feel he only accepts me for the sake of him keeping a relationship with his daughter, and I guess you can say I'm cool with that for now. Besides, it looks like he has to deal with me for a minute with the baby on the way and all.

As far as the Summer goes, despite the heat the police is bringing, Burger and Slim been holding the trap down. They're the ones making all the cheese, while everyone else sneaks in and out because of the heat. So by the time things do cool down, those two should be dam near millionaires.

Me and Slanga still waiting on that information from Firebug and Big Wade. They sent that little bit about them snitches and Singleton, but we really need that information on these agents. Slanga wanted to ask them to come and aid us, but like I told him, that's our beef, we can handle our own.

True enough we helped them, but he has to realize that we did that. It's not like they're gonna come and personally handle it like we did. If it does get to that level, they are just gonna send some cats that we know nothing about, and that really would have me more paranoid then the harassing cops.

The way I see it, every man has a conscience, and the way things are going out here, you catch more time for conspiring to murder, than the person who actually pulled the trigger. With that said, give me the pistol any day.

To tell the truth I really don't wanna do nothing but sit back until my birthday, which is only a few weeks away. I'm thinking about going down to Florida to holler at my peoples, just to get away for a few.

Now who the hell is this knocking on the door?

"Who is it?"

"Open the door, boo," I hear Teresa say from the other side.

173

STUCK

I should've took my ass to Savannah with Slanga, but I've promised her that we would spend some time together. She's been tripping lately, but who can really blame her. Hell, I haven't been really showing her any attention.

When I opened the door I noticed that she still had her uniform on.

"What are you doing off work so early?" I asked.

"Good afternoon to you too," she sarcastically replied as she walked past me into the suite.

"Teresa, stop tripping," I stated as I closed and locked the door behind her.

"You're the one that's tripping!" She stressed with her hand over her face before asking, "So when did you start back smoking?"

"Today," is all I managed to reply with.

"What's wrong, is everything alright? I mean is it something I done?" She stresses.

"Na'll playgirl, you didn't do nothing. I just wasn't expecting you here so soon," I replied as I sat on the edge of the bed.

"You must have your other lady friend coming over or something?" She implied with a questionable expression as she laid across the bed.

"If I did, I might as well call her and tell her she can't come now," I responded with a sly grin.

"You got that shit right! And don't get fucked up behind that bullshit!" She stressed before sitting erect on the bed.

What a major turn off. I ask myself all the time, how someone so beautiful could say stupid shit like that.

"Slow your roll," I stated openly agitated, "this is supposed to be our time, so let's not spoil it with the bickering."

"Your right," she replied before rising from the bed and adding, "let me take a quick shower."

I got mad love for Teresa, but she really ain't aiding the journey right now. And yeah, I'll be the first to admit, that it's far from being her fault. It's really kind of hard trying to balance time between the streets and two females, especially when one doesn't know about the other.

I wanna tell her to move back to the Sea-Port, but she ain't the type to take that too kindly right now. My heart truly pains me knowing that I'm the true culprit. So yeah I have feelings for her, but the fact still remains that I can't trust her to be completely down for a playa.

That cat David wrote me the other day, really threw me for a loop. The letter was in her mailbox in Savannah. Obviously, she'd mentioned the fact that I gave her that money, because buddy was thanking me for looking out. Out of respect of the game, is how wrote it, he gave me a little more insight on Teresa, and their situation.

I sent him my address here in Augusta and told him if he needed anything, hit me up. I also let him know that I didn't send that cheese on behalf of Teresa, I sent it for the sake of the struggle. He might understand, and he might not.

✱✱✱✱✱✱✱✱✱✱✱✱✱✱

Red and Black were slap boxing in the middle of the street while Georgia Slim and Hamburger looked on.

"I got a hundred on Black," Georgia Slim stressed to Hamburger.

"Bet that!" Hamburger retorted before calling out, "Say Red, you got fifty of this if you get the best of him."

Out of all the fellas, Red and Black were always the ones providing the physical entertainment. Every now and then they all would go at each other on the front porch, but things never got out of hand between them. They were all the family some of them knew.

"Say ya'll, there go Ms. Mildred!" Hamburger yelled out.

Ms. Mildred pulled up in her older model Fleetwood Cadillac. When she was finally close enough, she started yelling at Red and Black.

"Somebody just called and said to me, Mrs. Mildred, you got some dummies out here trying to kill each other!" She stressed after stopping in front of them.

"Now, Ms. Mildred, you should know better than that," Red replied while walking towards the car to open her door.

"I know boy!" She stressed as she stepped out of the car, "I wouldn't care about none of that, I really came by here because them police just left my house. They was trying to tell me that ya'll had something to do with them people they found dead."

"Oh yeah?!" Black grilled, "What else did they say?"

"I didn't give them a chance to say much of nothing," she replied as she rolled her eyes at him, "I told them to get off my property. Hell, if they think ya'll killed them people for talking too much, what the hell they think ya'll gonna do to me?" She added allowing the fellas to burst with laughter.

"Ms. Mildred, you know that ain't nobody gonna do nothing to you," Georgia Slim stated before jumping off the porch and adding, "if anything, they better be worried about you doing something to them."

"I'm just saying, ya'll need to be careful out here, cause they gonna try to do everything they can to lock ya'll up."

"Yes mamm," Hamburger replied as he saw Kruger jump out a yellow cab.

"Dam playboy, where you been?" Georgia Slim questioned.

"I had to see my parole officer yesterday, so I just took the rest of the day off," Kruger replied.

"Hey boy," Ms. Mildred yelled at Kruger, "you act as if you don't see me over here?"

"I didn't Ms. Mildred, how you doing?" He responded as he walked over and embraced her,

"So how much I owe you?"

"You don't owe me nothing baby," she replied with a huge grin on her face.

"How come you don't never curse him out like you do the rest of us?" Hamburger inquired.

"Shut up boy, you stay worried about the wrong thing!" She retorted before she looked over at Kruger and winked her eye.

Kruger returned her smile with one of his own before he looked over at Georgia Slim and stressed, "Say Slim let me holler at you for a minute."

"What's going playboy?" Georgia Slim asked.

"How everything been going down here?"

"Shit been running kind of smooth every since you hollered at your girl peoples. I guess you can say they been looking somebody else they can point the finger at," Georgia Slim replied before pausing a moment and adding, "But Ms. Mildred did just say that the oppressor just left her house asking questions. But you know she don't know nothing, so what can she say."

"True," Kruger agreed.

"But as far as this cheddar go, I got like two

179

left from what I got from you, but I should be done with that tonight."

"You and Burger have been stacking that bread, huh?"

"We just taking advantage of the opportunity," he replied with a light smile.

"Playboy, I won't feel right until everybody on the Summer at least have a brick of their own, so I'm glad that ya'll handling things." Kruger stated as they stopped on the corner of Summer and Hopkins Street, "but on a whole nother level, I'm thinking about hitting Miami for my b-day. I just wanted you to know so that you can have your money right."

"You know I'm down, but when you planning on leaving?"

"It's on Friday, the 17th, but we probably leave that Monday, and if we do, we ain't coming back to the following Monday. So if you wanna take a female, that's cool too. Because you know nine times out of ten, I'm taking Deidra."

"Yeah, that's cool too, because I got this tight stallion in College Park I wouldn't mind exposing on that journey."

"It don't matter," Kruger replied before

180

adding, "I'm gonna get at everybody and let them know what's good. But I had to holler at you first, because I know I want you there."

-TERESA-

"So, how the hell is he gonna do some shit like that?" I was asking Toya as we sat on her couch watching re-runs of Martin.

"Girl you know your man better than me, but maybe he just wanna get away for his birthday," she replied with.

You know a lot of times I can't really tell whose side she really on.

"I'm just saying, he should at least take me!" I retorted.

She just looked over at me and rolled her eyes before saying, "First of all, you can't take any more days off. And on top of all that, all of his friends are going and you know that you don't like being around them."

"Dam that!" I snapped back, "The only reason that you're so cool with it is Ron ain't going."

"Girl, you know that those two are the total opposite!" She stated openly aggravated, "Ron works and goes to school while you're around here pretending that you don't know that Deamon is back hustling!"

"I know, I just don't want to believe it."

"He's just like Eddie and David!" She stated as she raised from the couch and headed toward the bathroom, "You need to find you a square, and stop putting yourself in the same fucked up position."

I try not to pay her any attention, because I know that she's going in her fifth month of pregnancy, so she's always cranky. It ain't my fault that she went from a size 9 to a size 14. But despite that, she's right, but what am I really suppose to do about it?

I mean, I can't think of anyone else that I would rather be with. When I'm with him, it's like I feel whole. I know he slips at times, but when I told him that I felt he was neglecting our relationship, he stepped right up and made things right.

It's like whenever I bring certain things to his attention that I'm uncomfortable with, he at least shows enough concern to attempt to rectify the problem or whatever.

But now he's leaving for Miami Monday, without me. That really irks the hell out of me for many reasons. I mean I can't believe that he's not gonna spend his birthday with me. To me that's like our anniversary, and he wants to spend that with his friends?

I mean we rarely spend time together as it is, so I truly hate spoiling the little time we do have together with my bickering. But dam, he has to hear how this trip without me, makes me feel.

-KRUGER-

"What's going playboy?" Slanga was asking..

"Say homie, I need you to take Kay-Kay an eighth, cause she's about out," he replied before pausing and adding, "I got you when I get back in town."

"Consider it done. Anything else you need?"

"Na'll, everything is everything. Just make sure you keep your phone on cause I'm gonna tell her to call you within the hour."

"Alright playboy, just be safe on your way back."

"That's what's up, but you know I'm bringing Amanda with me so that we don't have to swing this way on our way to Miami."

"I'll see ya'll when you get here."

"Much love playboy."

"Til death!" I retorted before I pushed the end button.

Here I am just riding through the city enjoying the moment and this fool calls me with a task. It's all good though, that's my peoples.

It wasn't even ten minutes later that my phone rings with Kay-Kay on the other end.

"What's up ole sexy black ass nigga?" She asked.

Now, I ain't about to front, but shortie had me grinning. I've been so strung out with other shit, that I had forgot how tempting she is.

"What's popping?"

"Do you know how long I've been trying to get this number?" She said.

Now I'm dam near blushing, and I'm glad her ass was on that other end of this phone. As much as I'm hate to admit it, Kay-Kay got a playa attention.

"So now that you have it, what are you gonna do with it?" I questioned.

One thing I can't see is, me throwing myself to no woman. Ain't no difference in her and any other woman, so she has to fight for a position just like the rest of them.

"Can a bitch buy you dinner?" Is what I hear her ask.

Her boldness can be a pro or a con, but for right now, it's a definite pro.

"Yeah, right after we take care of that little business!"

Business before all that other shit!

"I have no problem with that," is all she replied with.

"Well, give me like forty-five minutes," I stated.

"If it's gonna take you that long, you might as well pick me up at my mama's house in Allen Homes. That gives me time to freshen up."

"Just be sitting on the porch."

"Bye sexy," she stated in a devious tone.

"Forty-five minutes!" I stressed before hanging up.

STUCK

I guess you can say that she's finally about to get what she's been asking for. I'm suppose to swing through and holler at Teresa, but I'll just call and tell her that we'll get together tomorrow. We have to talk anyway.

I need to call Deidra and tell her to bring me one of those sacks, since I have everything wrapped in eighths anyway.

"Hello," Deidra stated after the second ring.

"What are you doing?"

"Throwing up everywhere. Deamon, I think this baby is trying to kill me."

"Do you need me to come and take you to the hospital?" I asked with sincere concern.

Man, I really don't know what to do when shit like this go down. That's the only part of all this I'm afraid of.

"Na'll, I think that I'll be alright," she replied as I heard the toilet flush.

I could tell that she was smiling. I learned a long time ago that when it comes down to women, all it takes is for a playa to show that he cares, nothing more, nothing less.

"Baby-girl, come to the door," I stated after pulling in the driveway.

186

"Deamon, I know that you're not outside?" She asked as if it was impossible.

"Girl, if you don't come to this door!"

Twenty minutes later I was headed to Allen Homes. When I pulled up in front of Kay- Kay's mama's apartment, she was sitting on the porch. She had on a soft pink summer dress that fit her perfectly. I could tell that she had on thongs because her ass was jiggling too freely. I gave her the pack and she took it in the house. Five minutes later we were headed towards Washington Road.

"You must have really never wanted to get at me?" She asked after turning down the sounds of Jay-Z's, "You Must Love Me".

"It ain't like that, I've just been on some other shit lately," I replied.

"You should already know that I'm on point, I just wanted to see what you had to say," she confessed with a sly grin.

If you ask me, she's almost too cocky with it.

"Even a blind muthafucka can see what's really happening out here," She added, "I ain't trying to say that ya'll did it or nothing, but whoever knocked off those snitches, did the game a favor. And I say that, even though one of those muthafuckas was my second cousin."

I looked over at her and saw her in a whole different dimension. Some may say that I'm crazy or whatever, but what just came out her mouth, to me, just made her thirty times sexier.

"I see why Slanga keeps you around like he does. It seems that you have a little sense with that cute face."

She just blushed, "You ain't so bad yourself."

We rode in silence for a moment before she suggested, "Kruger, let's just say fuck dinner, and get a room, on me."

"I really don't know about all of that," I replied in a suave manner.

"What the fuck do you mean?"!"

"I mean, the rooms I usually stay in are a hundred or better," I replied with a sly grin.

This made her blush before she stressed, "For you, I'll come off a grand."

"I can dig that, but we still have to get something to eat and stop by the liquor store."

"You mean to tell me that you have to be

drunk to get this?" She questioned as she grabbed my free hand and placed it in that spot between her legs.

Man, was she wet! You wouldn't think that it would be like that, but dam, it was.

"Dam shortie," is all I was able to say before easing my hand away.

Dam, what a mood changer! She had pushed me to the wall just that fast. I turned back up the music in an attempt to take what she had just did off of my mind. This woman was too tempting, but being who I was, I just couldn't let her know that.

I stopped at *Fazzoli's* and ordered two sampler platters and two half subs. When I pulled up at the liquor store, she went in and stayed for about three minutes before rushing out.

"I hope you're smoking," she stressed as she tossed a box of Swishers at me.

"I get down every now and then," was my response as I pulled out of the parking-lot.

Twenty minutes later we were walking inside of our room of Homewood Suites.

"Why you looking like that, Ms. So Anxious?" I asked after seeing the unfamiliar expression on her face.

"You know I have never been in a room like this," she stated with a shocked expression.

"I guess it's a first time for everything," I stressed as I sat on the edge of the king sized bed, "if you pay forty Jugs for a room, you'll get forty Jugs worth, sometimes even less than that."

She walked over and sat next to me before she kissed me on the cheek and stated, "Thank-you, for bringing me here."

"You tripping, you must done forgot that you're the one who paid for this."

"That's not the point."

"What's the point then?" I asked her, because sometimes a playa just has to see where their heads at.

"The point is, you just raised my cost of living. After this, tell me how can I settle for Days Inn?"

"I can feel you on that, but you're making enough bread to raise your own standards," I replied as I raised from the bed and grabbed the food.

"Man, you know that Slanga is making all the money, and me and Prime is just getting pimped," is what she stated in a frustrated manner.

"Now, you have to know that you're violating right now!" I retorted with a little more emotions then needed, "You and Prime should be discussing that with Slanga, not me!"

"You right, but that still ain't gonna make shit right," Kay-Kay stated as she looked at me with a quizzical expression.

"Slanga my peoples, and if he's wrong or right, I'm with him. None of this has nothing to do with me. Just like you told me in the car, you're already on point," is what I indicated, just to let her know that on my behalf there isn't any leaks in me and my man's bond.

"Like I said, my bad," she replied with a phony smile before adding, "we don't even suppose to be on this level anyway."

Her phony smile just let me know that I can't do anything with her but knock her off.

We basically ate in silence. It really bothered me that she would try me like she just had. To me, it seems that her motive was to join my team, and that only meant that she was really unhappy with hers. And everybody with sense knows, that an unhappy person on your team, is the best inside source, for outside interference.

191

STUCK

I wonder if she's so blind that she doesn't realize that she's already well established with my team. Now if she does realize it, she must feel that if she dealt with me she'll move up in rank. Dam, if she feels like that, I must appear to be the weak link.

True indeed, the power of pussy would make a lot of cats commit a lot of foolish deeds, but I never thought you could put a playa like myself in that position. It's death before dishonor, and with that said, how can I cross that line!

Man, I can sit here and ask myself question after question and never come up with any concrete answers. The only way for me to find out her true motives is to play the game out.

"So what color panties do you have on?" Is what I finally asked as if I've been wondering for the longest.

"I don't wear panties, I wear thongs," is what she stressed as she rose from her seat and walked towards the bed before implying, "if you wanna find out so bad, come find out for yourself."

"Why you ain't roll that blunt up?" I asked as I grabbed the bottle of *Hennessy* she'd bought.

"While you was sitting there in a world of your own I was rolling it," is what she replied before taking the blunt from her ear and lighting it up.

She really caught me off guard with what she had asked next, "Have you ever got head while smoking on some chocolate-tye?"

"Not lately," is all I was able to reply with.

"Well, come here and bring that bottle with you," she stressed in a seductive tone as she stretched out on the bed.

Thirty minutes later her head rested on my chest. I had to admit that she was beyond ready. The way she climbed on top, I knew I was in for a helluva ride. It's like she had mastered the art of seduction, because she definitely had me wide open. Any position that came to mind, we experienced. She was definitely above a ten on the sex scale.

"Are you alright?" Is what she asked me as she lightly raked her fingers across my chest.

"Yeah, I'm good," I nonchalantly replied.

"I'm glad that I could put a smile on your face," is what she stressed.

"You talk as if you're done for the night," is what I stressed as I looked over at her.

"Dam, you're trying to put a bitch out of

commission?" Is what she asked with a light smile.

"Now, you're talking as if you're scared or something?" I questioned before sarcastically asking, "Now, I know Ms. So Anxious ain't scared?"

"Don't try to bring that scared game to the table with me," she stressed as I eased over her and lifted her leg over my shoulder.

"You act as if this our last time," she practically moaned out.

I just leaned over and nibbled on her ear before whispering, "Never put off tomorrow what you could do today."

With that said she grabbed me and guided me inside her.

Dam! I never met a woman who could get so wet!

Our first session was like a grudge match. I guess we were trying to get the feel of each other. This time is more intensified. It's like she put her hard-core image to the side and allowed herself to enjoy the moment.

As I penetrated at a slow pace, I have to admit that her facial expressions excited me more than her eagerness to meet my every stroke. There was no secret that she had won round one, but I was determined to win round two.

I grabbed her right leg and placed it over my left shoulder. I never rushed it, I wanted her to feel all of me. She lightly raked my back with her nails as she let out soft whimpers. She started to press her nails harder into my back, so I grabbed her hands and pinned them to the bed.

"What you trying to do to me?" Is what she stuttered out.

"The same thing you was trying to do to me," I replied in a hoarse manner.

She closed her eyes and squeezed my hand tighter while letting out a deep moan, right before her body went limp under me. It only took me a few more strokes before I joined her in ecstasy.

I eventually rolled over on the side of her and kissed her on the cheek before I finally asked, "Are you alright, baby-girl?"

She looked over at me and practically whispered, "You have to be the devil or something, cause my body just felt possessed."

"Dam, a good nut gets you to talking like that?" Is what I questioned with a smile of approval.

195

"Get away from me!" Was how she retorted as she slid out of the bed and headed towards the bathroom.

Seeing that ass sashay towards the bathroom only aroused me more, "Kay-Kay."

"What?" Is how she replied in a nasty manner.

"Chill baby-girl," I smoothly stated, "a good nut does that to us all."

"Well, it ain't never did me like that!" Is what she stressed as she walked in the bathroom and closed the door behind her.

I sat up and grabbed the half of blunt that we had put out earlier, and lit it back up. I then poured me a glass of cognac and turned the television on.

After flipping through the channels, I realized why I never watched the trick box. Luckily after a few moments I found the movie Scarface on. It was about 2:30 in the morning and Tony had just found some chico trying to make out with his sister in the bathroom. The moment Tony slapped his sister, Kay-Kay was walking out of the bathroom.

I passed her the blunt and she took a few

pulls before saying, "I'm sorry, I guess I acted like a kid."

"Like I told you before you went in there, that you was straight." I replied with a light smile before adding, "Shit happens. It don't always be what happened, but who it happened with."

"I just hope that I haven't scared you away."

"Only time will tell," I replied before I went for round three.

(CHAPTER 7)

-KRUGER-

*"**Who was** that?"* Pimp was asking after I hung my phone up.

Me and him are sitting in the middle room of the boarding house playing chess.

"That was Weasey," I answered before adding, "he said he's about to ride through.

"I tried to holler at that cat the other day, but he never answered his phone."

"He say they been out of town," I revealed as he pushed one of his pieces.

"Oh yeah," Pimp quizzed, "they should be straight then?"

"Dam playboy, we straight!" I stressed, "I know that's your people and all, but we got it right here on the Summer. We got it so that a nigga ain't gotta move outside these walls to get right."

"If ya'll was here all the time, then I probably could fuck with ya'll like that!" he retorted.

I just shook my head in disgust, "Man, don't

198

play yourself like that, cause if you really wanted something from us, then you know how to find us."

"I know my nigga," he replied with that ole funny smirk, "but you know that it's always good to have a outside connect."

"Look playboy, I ain't trying to be funny or nothing, but sometimes that outside force be the one to destroy you."

"True, but you know that's Weasey," Pimp replied before adding, "and you of all people should know that most of the time it be your inside niggas who get you."

I just gave him a smirk, "Say no more, but let me make this clear, it ain't Weasel who I'm concerned with, it's that cat Jimmy."

"Man, that nigga don't know shit about us, but what we want him to know!" Pimp retorted.

"Peep game playboy," I stressed, "when those cats fall by the waste side, whoever is dealing with them might as well pack up too. Besides, ole boy got a chip on his shoulder with me behind that broad."

"Yeah, I can see that at times."

"Any naked eye could see that! Now Weasel, you know that's my dog, but he knows what's going with buddy. You have to realize that Weasel ain't moving that shit by himself, you best believe that Jimmy knows about every deal he makes and vice-versa.

All I'm saying big bra, is if you're gonna deal with them, be ready to either do time or execute them." I continued, "But all I'm trying to tell you is, all that can be avoided."

"Yeah, I can see where you coming from," Pimp responded as he moved his bishop from in front of his king.

"Just think about it, and while you're thinking about that," I stated as I moved my queen next to Pimp's king, "think about this checkmate."

"Dam!" Pimp spat out as he raised from his chair and headed towards the front door.

I just sat there for a moment pondering on the conversation.

The way I see it, this fool caught some animosity from somewhere, I just can't pin-point the source right now. I know Weasel his cousin, but it's a lot deeper than that. It's sad because now I have to keep an eye on him. All I can remember is what Big Wade said about once you catch that awkward feeling.

I'm in desperate need of getting away from all this shit, so I can't wait for Monday to get here. It ain't just Pimp and these everyday struggles in the street either, Teresa tripping too.

She around here talking about we should be together for my birthday. To her my birthday is like some sort of anniversary for us. She stay trying to clog my brain with shit I have no time for. I'm about to let her know that I'm back grinding, something I already know she knows. My thing is, maybe she'll understand it better when I explain it to her.

It ain't gonna be easy letting go of that sexy green eyed bandit, but her time is quickly running out. Every day I lose more and more respect for her and gain more and more for Deidra.

Now Deidra is like the ideal hustler's mate, but to be honest, I'm afraid if I show her too much love she'll only start taking advantage of it.

And that's the only reason I don't go that extra mile with her. Sound stupid don't it?

But like this old man told me when I was locked up, you have to have patience and give everything time to air out, but stay focused. That old man knew patience better than anyone I know. He had already done twenty-seven years and still had thirteen more to go.

"Say Kruger," Burger called me from the porch.

"Yeah, what up?" I walked down the hall towards the front door.

"Man, Weasel out here stunting with the top down!"

When I stepped on the porch, all I could see was the sun shining off of that fresh candy burgundy paint and sitting on all that rim.

I'm tripping because I was just on the phone with this cat while he was picking his car up from the rim shop, so he knows that I have this Tahoe I'm bringing out.

But I gotta admit this cat out here really stunting with this convertible. When he called me and told me what he was riding in, I told him that he better try to shine before my birthday, because that's when I'm bringing that Tahoe to the table.

"Dam playboy, I see that you have started without me," I said as I walked to the convertible.

"Playboy, I heed all warnings," he said with a wide grin, "you told me to shine while I can, so bling muthafuckin bling!"

"Where you headed?" I asked him.

"Nigga, if you don't get in, you know that I have to holler at you," he replied.

Right after I jumped in, I noticed that there was no music. Hell, there wasn't even a deck. "Dam playboy, where the music at?"

"That's where I'm headed now. They already done hooked everything else up, all they have to do now is put the disc player in and tune everything. It shouldn't take no more than fifteen or twenty minutes."

"That's cool," I replied.

Pimp walked over to the car and asked Weasel, "Say cousin, how long ya'll gonna be?"

"No more than an hour," Weasel replied before pulling off.

After a few moments of silence he asked me, "What's up with that nigga Pimp?"

"What you mean?" I replied with a questionable expression.

"I mean that nigga ain't getting money like the rest of ya'll. It's like he's content with coping a big eighth."

I couldn't help but chuckle before replying with, "Hell, that's your cousin, and you don't know, so tell me how am I suppose to answer that?"

203

"I know he likes hitting the clubs and hotels with them freaks and shit, but."

"Playboy, you already know me!" I interrupted with a serious expression.

This dude is really tripping right now. See sometimes you just have to kill the bullshit, cause some cats will never take you serious if you always smiling and joking around.

"When it comes to another man's pocket, I mind my own," I assured him, "I mean, I can show a nigga the door, but it's on him to open it."

"That's the same way I feel," he replied with a relieved expression, "I just wanted to know if I was wrong for feeling that way."

"Man, stop tripping!" I stressed in total disbelief.

I know this cat like the back of my hand, and I really can't believe that he just tried to play with my intelligence.

"Now, who am I to judge the way you feel?" I questioned, "Playboy, you know better than to worry about how another dude feels about your way of thinking."

He just smiled at my outburst before he himself replied with, "The reason I asked is the nigga been getting lovely prices, but he ain't coming up. The fool insist to continue to ree-up with the same little 2,600."

"Playboy, everybody don't hustle the same," I replied before taking a deep breath, "You can't look to get the same amount of milk out of every cow, but you already know that. See you know just like I know that this Pimp shit ain't the real issue you want to speak on, so go ahead and spit it out."

"Dam homie, you don't let shit get by, do you?" He reacted with a sly grin.

"You know, I try to stay on everything that needs my attention, but since I'm only human, every now and then I tend to neglect something," I replied.

"But, if you insist, I wanted to get at you about that broad Surina," he asked as if it was an everyday question for us.

"What about her?" I probably replied with a little too much emotion.

Man, I hope this fool ain't striving to put me in a situation that I know him and his people can't handle.

"The nigga Jimmy think that she had

something to do with this pack that got missing a few months back," he finally revealed.

"He thinks she did it or do you think she did it?" I cross-examined with an expression that told him that I already knew the answer.

"Both of us really think that she did," he indicated in a tone as if he was trying to tell me that he was still his own man.

I couldn't help but smile before asking, "So what does all that have to do with me, bra?"

"I'm just letting you know because if we find out she did do it, we still have to stick to the G-Code." Is what he had the nerve to say.

"Playboy, let this be heard loud and clear!" I blasted, "Surina is no longer with me, she's your man's broad. And if she has violated ya'll in anyway, that's on him, not me. I mean, really, who am I to even give an opinion on this?"

"I can feel that. Look bra, Jimmy don't know that we're having this conversation, so this between me and you."

"Playboy, I appreciate and cherish the respect you have for a playa, I mean you have to know that I sincerely do. But in this game you have to have some sort of limit to everything. For example, if Jimmy violates and it can't be paid off, do you actually think that I'm gonna talk to you about it before I make my move?"

****

"Anyone of ya'll see Kruger?" Gunslanga asked after pulling in front of 1122 in his Lincoln.

"Yeah, he riding around with Weasel," Hamburger replied from his normal spot on the porch.

"They should be on their way back," Pimp added, "hit them up and see where they at."

Gunslanga grabbed his phone and called Kruger.

"Yeah," Kruger answered after the third ring.

"Fool, where you at?"

"We turning on Summer now."

"Yeah, I see ya'll." Gunslanga stated before hanging up the phone and getting out the car.

After the Caprice pulled next to Gunslanga's Lincoln, Weasel was the first to speak.

"The Notorious Gunslanga!" Is what he practically screamed over the sounds of 2-Pac's, "Death Around The Corner".

"What's going Weasy, I see you ain't cutting no corners with The Chevy game," Gunslanga disclosed.

"I'm just trying to beat you to the punch," Weasel clarified.

"Well you know that I'm a Cadillac man myself, so I'm gonna let you have this here."

"I preciate that, big homie."

"Where ya'll fools been anyway?" Gunslanga asked as Kruger made his way out of the car.

"Just riding and looking for fresh meat," Weasel replied with a wide grin.

"NIgga, speak for yourself!" Kruger stated after closing the car door.

Weasel just shook his head and chuckled before saying, "I guess I'll see ya'll a little later."

All the fellas watched as Pimp walked over to the Caprice and jumped in the passenger seat right before Weasel pulled off.

"I guess we won't see him until the

morning," Hamburger declared from the porch.

"That's probably a little too early for him," Red argued.

"The nigga still don't know that you can't get no cheese riding all over the city," Black added.

"Well, that's just how the story goes for ole Pimp," Gunslanga pointed out.

"Man, dam that! Is ya'll niggas ready to make that trip to the bottom?" Kruger interjected.

"And you already know!" Hamburger stressed.

"I don't think that I'm gonna be able to make that trip," Black revealed.

"What up?" Gunslanga petitioned, "You need some help with something?"

"Na'll, it's my niece's birthday next week, so I gotta handle that," he replied.

Gunslanga just looked over at Kruger with a disturbing expression before saying, "Man check this, buy her a bike and when we get back, we'll all pitch in and throw her a party at *Chuke Cheese*."

"Say no more!" Black excitedly responded.

"Anyone of ya'll see Slim?" Kruger asked.

"He out there in Meadowbrook with shortie

209

from College Park," Red replied before adding, "but you know he riding."

"So since everything all good, we pulling out Monday morning," Kruger stated before him an Gunslanga started to walk down the street.

"What that fool Weasel talking about?" Gunslanga asked after they were a few feet from 1122.

"Nothing really," Kruger replied before implying, "You remember I told you that Surina hit them cats for that quarter."

"Yeah fool, I remember."

"Well, he telling me that they think she did it. And if they found out she did do it, they gotta take her head off."

"So why he hit you with that noise?" Gunslanga questioned.

"Cause they know that she gave it to me, but they're too scared to ask," he answered with a sly grin.

"Oh yeah," Gunslanga stated with a chuckle of his own before implying, "But dam that! You know I still owe you that eighth with Kay-Kay. You want it now or when we get back from the bottom?"

"Man, you know that shit can wait."

"I just wanted you to know that I ain't forgot about it."

Kruger just smiled at his comrade before replying with, "You already know I already know where we stand. But, my main concern right now is this cat Pimp. I really just realized that we have to keep an eye on his ass."

"Nigga, I've been doing that, so you're the one that's slipping!" He replied with a disturbing expression.

"So why you ain't put me on point?" Kruger questioned.

"I thought that you were already aware of your surroundings?"

Kruger just shook his head and stressed, "He just been acting shady lately. We were just playing chess and I had a word with him about dealing with Jimmy and Weasel. And it wasn't even about what he was saying either, it was really how he was reacting."

"What you ask him?"

"I asked him, why he always waiting on Jimmy them when we got it right here."

"Jealousy is a muthafucka!" Gunslanga spat

out before adding, "This fool done been out here all this time, while we been locked-up. Now we done got out, and we working with more cheese than him."

"Na'll playboy," Kruger replied in disbelief.

"You must owe the nigga something?" He questioned.

"I don't think so."

"Well, I know I don't!" Gunslanga retorted before taking a deep breath and adding, "Matter of fact, all we have been is good to the crab."

"Well, he know if he needs something and I got it, it ain't nothing for me to give it to him."

"That's just the fool's pride, if you ask me. Just keep your eyes and ears open for right now. Hopefully he'll get his money up to the point where he is comfortable enough to let that air out. But, if he trips before that happens, then.."

"What's understood doesn't need to be talked about!" Kruger stressed while soaking in the reality of the conversation.

"I know how you feel bra," he stressed after seeing the disturbed look on Kruger's face, "but you know just as well as I do, that there's rules to this shit."

"You know I know, I'm just hoping that this fool knows it too. I'll just hate for this nigga to find out the hard way."

"But fuck that, cause it is what it is with him," he stated before a smirk appeared on his face, "What I want to know is what did you tell Teresa about Miami?"

"What you mean?"

"I mean, I know that she didn't take that news to lightly."

"Yeah, she tripped, but I promised her a trip to Charlotte next month," he replied as they walked past Gunslanga's house and towards Dyess Park.

"Dam, baby-boy getting very expensive with a factory salary," he joked.

"I am, ain't I," he replied with a quizzical expression before adding, "I'm thinking about going ahead and telling her."

"Oh yeah?" Gunslanga asked as if he already knew it was coming.

"Yeah, but I don't think that I'm prepared for all that emotional shit."

"You know, she gonna be subject to run off with some square after you tell her that."

"Yeah, but if it goes down, it just goes down," he replied in a sadden tone.

Gunslanga realized that his comrade wasn't feeling that conversation at all so he asked, "Where Deidra at?"

"She most likely still showing Amanda around," he replied with a smile before adding, "you know they been kicking it real strong lately."

"Yeah, I even know that she's walking around here carrying your seed," Gunslanga revealed.

"Dam, they getting too close then!" He replied in a shocked manner.

"Don't sweat that because it might be a good thing," he stated before adding, "you know them two can relate to each other after dealing with niggas like us."

"I feel ya, but.."

"But nothing," he interjected, "it ain't like she running around here talking about who you done killed or where your stash at. She told a close friend that she was pregnant. Lighten up pimp, you have to give her some breathing room."

"You might be right."

"I know I'm right, cause she'll do anything in

214

the world for her Deamon. But I ain't telling you nothing that you don't already know," he implied as they walked on the basketball court.

"Now that's genuine right there," Kruger replied with a smile.

"Now, I just wished that we had a ball, so that I could take some of your money," he declared.

"Playboy, you know you wasn't looking to see me," Kruger revealed as they made their way back up Summer Street.

(CHAPTER 8)

Dyess Park was packed with young hustlers from all over the 9th Street area. While they were on the basketball court, their women were on the sidelines gossiping among each other. It was Sunday afternoon and Deidra, Amanda and Georgia Slim's College girl, Vikki, sat on the bleachers, in their summer dresses, away from the other women.

Most of their conversation consisted of Deidra showing them who was who, until Vikki asked Deidra, "Girl, how do you do it?"

"Do what?" Deidra questioned with a confused expression.

"Share your man with another woman," Vikki questioned in a disgusted manner.

Amanda cut in and answered the question before Deidra had the chance to, "She don't care nothing about that, and besides that other girl ain't gonna be there too much longer."

"She right," Deidra revealed, "all that other woman stuff don't bother me, cause I'm the only one who knows what he needs and wants."

"I guess you're right," Vikki finally agreed, "cause you're in a better position with the baby on the way and all."

That statement hit a nerve with Deidra, but she held her composure and replied with, "I don't want him to be with me because of the baby. I want him to love me for being his backbone."

"So what you're saying is, you're his rib?" Vikki joked.

"Definitely!" Deidra stressed with a wide grin, "And I ain't going nowhere."

"Deidra," Vikki called out as her eyes were focused on the parking lot, "Who's that pulling up with the top down?"

After seeing who she was asking about she replied with, "Oh that's Weasel. He use to be on the Summer too, until he moved to the county and hooked up with this nigga name Jimmy."

"Who's Jimmy?" Amanda asked.

"You'll see in a minute, that's him in the black car behind the vert."

Weasel parked his car on the grass so that everyone could see it. In the passenger seat was a female who wore a burgundy wig that matched his paint. After she stepped out, she went right to Jimmy's passenger door.

"And that's Surina," Deidra uttered out as if her entire day was just spoiled.

Surina walked towards the bleachers as if she was walking down the runway, modeling her attire. Her white Capri pants turned every head on the court, even Kruger's. And no one knew that he was watching her better than Deidra. Her eyes were fixed on him to see his reaction. She noticed that it took him three double takes before he finally brushed her off.

As she walked past the court Surina looked over at Kruger and winked her eye, before she stepped over to Deidra.

"Hey ladies, how are ya'll doing?" Surina greeted as if she was a queen showing love to her people, "I'm Surina and this is Ericka."

Everyone spoke except Deidra, who just glanced at Ericka and shook her head before raising from her seat and saying, "Amanda and Vikki, I'll be over by the court watching the game."

"Deidra, do you mind if I have a few words with you?" Surina asked.

Deidra glared at her before rolling her eyes

and walking away.

"Deidra!" She called out again.

Deidra paid her no mind as she continued to walk towards the basketball court.

****

Weasel was talking more trash than usual, while him and Jimmy sat on the sideline waiting for next. They had already gave the dude who had next fifty dollars for his downs.

Gunslanga, Georgia Slim, Red, Kruger and this other cat that went by the name Ugly-O had already won three games and was one point away from winning their fourth.

Ugly-O was another cat getting money in the 9th Street area. He was just a few blocks away on Carrie Street.

"Man, I can't believe that ya'll got Ugly-O on the team," Weasel was on the sideline taunting.

Just when he said that, Ugly-O hit a ten foot jumper and looked over at Weasel with a golden smile and stated, "Now bet something!"

"Make it light on yourself, big homie,"

STUCK

Weasel replied with a sinister grin.

"A dollar a man and ya'll can go and get Shaq and Kobe," Gunslanga stressed.

Jimmy obviously felt that it was time to make his presence known because he stressed, "Make that two dollars a man and we pick up Sam, Jeff and Derrick."

All three of the cats he named played high school ball, but now they were hustling in the 9th Street area.

Since they were now gambling everyone agreed that they should shot for first ball. Georgia Slim shot and hit, nothing but net.

"What we going to?" Jimmy asked.

"Eight," Kruger replied before adding, "we want this over with as quick as possible."

"Eight, it is then," Jimmy replied with his eyes focused on Kruger.

Kruger could tell that, to Jimmy, this game was worth more than the 200 dollars they were playing for, so he looked over at him and said, "Make sure you guard me."

They all matched up. Jeff on Gunslanga, Derrick on Georgia Slim, Sam on Red and Weasel on Ugly-O. Kruger took the ball out and passed it to

Ugly-O, who hit a jumper from the top of the key.

"Shoot another one, I got the rebound if you miss," Gunslanga stressed.

Kruger passed Ugly-O the ball again, but instead of him shooting, Kruger came around and set a pick on Weasel and rolled off. Ugly-O passed it to him, but Jeff saw the play all the way through, and pulled on Kruger. Kruger than threw an alley to Gunslanga, who caught it perfectly, causing the spectators to go wild. The game ended thirty minutes later, eight to five.

"Ya'll niggas just was already warmed up," Weasel stressed, "I would say bet back, but it feels like my heart is about to beat out of my chest."

"Too many smoke sessions little homie," Gunslanga stressed.

"Ya'll fools know that ya'll couldn't beat us anyway," Ugly-O pointed out.

"We'll, win the next time," Jimmy declared.

"Just make sure ya'll bring your A game," Georgia Slim inquired.

"True," Jimmy responded as he made his way towards his car before asking, "Say, ya'll want a brew, I got some in the trunk?"

"I preciate it playboy, but I got a few things

to take care of," Kruger replied before he called for Deidra.

Ten minutes later they were in her car headed to their hotel room.

"Do you know that Surina tried to talk to me back there?" Deidra implied as if she couldn't believe it.

"Oh yeah, what did you say to her?"

"I didn't say anything to her ass, I just walked away."

"You know that I don't feel comfortable about giving my opinion on you and her," he stated as she pulled in the hotel's parking-lot.

"I know you don't, but if I don't talk to you, who am I gonna talk to?"

"My bad," he replied as he stepped out of the car, "I never looked at it like that."

"So do you think that I should've talked to her?" She asked as she grabbed her purse out of the trunk.

"What do you think?" He asked as they walked towards the lobby doors.

She just shook her head before she replied with, "I think she should just stick to her thing and let me stick to mine."

"Well, that's what I feel you should've told her," he implied as he opened the door for her.

They really didn't say anything else until they walked into their hotel suite and he noticed that she looked a little distance, "You alright baby-girl?"

"Yeah, I'm alright," she replied while putting her purse on the table, "I just can't wait to get away from here for a minute."

He just smiled because he knew exactly where she was coming from, so he walked over to her and kissed her on the forehead before stressing, "We leave in the morning, so be patient."

-TERESA-

Deamon and his so-called homies suppose to be leaving for the airport in the morning, so me and Toya cooking for him and Ron tonight. I guess you can say that I wanna make sure my man eats before he leaves.

I am highly upset with his ass right now, because I've been sitting here waiting for over an hour. His ass has left me over here by myself with

223

the ghetto version of the Queen of England and her future husband, who acts as if he praises the ground she walks on.

I ain't gonna front, I'm really envious of how Toya and Ron be in here with the lovey dubby all day, while my so called man is in the streets everyday hustling his way back to prison. Yeah, his ass finally told me he's back out there. Of course I tripped, but if you think about it, what can you really say to someone who's up to their neck in mischief.

I honestly don't know why niggas feel that they are that one out of a million drug dealer that is gonna get away. You would think that after they get caught the first time, they'd learn their lesson. But these fools out here actually feel that they have got smarter at the shit or something.

"Teresa, get the door for your baby," Toya stressed as her and Ron laid all over each other on the couch.

I just stuck my tongue out at here and walked towards the door.

"You mad at me baby-girl?" Is what he asked as he handed me a red rose.

"Not anymore," I replied before giving him a passionate kiss.

After we finally separated, he walked in and spoke to Toya and his brother before heading for my room.

"Deamon, get back up here!" Is what I yelled before adding, "If we go back there, we'll never eat dinner."

"And you know with your freaky ass, that ain't nothing but the truth," Toya managed to giggled out.

"Toya stop all that hating," is what my baby said to her.

"Watch your mouth bra," Ron jumped to her defense.

"Ms. Lady, do you mind if I wash my hands before we eat?" Deamon asked me with a sly grin.

I just looked up at him and shook my head because I knew that he was up to no good.

"I might as well wash my hands too," I stated as I followed him to the bathroom.

As soon as we finished washing our hands, he was all over me. I mean, we just was washing our hands and the next thing I knew we were sprawled out over my bed as naked as the day we were born. For some strange reason I looked over at the clock on my nightstand and it read 8:27pm.

STUCK

Now this dude has gave me some of that unforgettable tongue before, but tonight he was going at it like he was possessed, because he literally had me in another dimension. I knew that Toya and Ron heard us back here, because he had my ass screaming.

I attempted to make my presence known as I rode that dick, but he was sucking on my nipples like I had just birth him, so I couldn't concentrate.

"Deamon, I'm cummmming!" Is what I managed to stutter out, before I collapsed on top of him.

He was still hard as a rock deep inside me, so after a few moments he maneuvered us so that he was on top. After realizing the position he had me in, I wrapped my lips around his left nipple and sucked on it as he started to plunge in and out of me. Now, I knew that I couldn't take the extra nipple attention, but he was far worse than me.

"Stop!" He managed to whisper out.

I ignored his ass and kept on doing me as I continued to meet his every stroke.

Now what really got him, was when I started raking his back with my nails. I don't know if it turned him on to know that I was feeling him like that or what, but his ass really started feeding me that dick.

I finally took my mouth from his nipple so that I could look into his face. I thought I was in another world, but this cat was definitely far from earth. I stared at him for a moment before I pushed him off me.

Without saying a word, I got on my hands and knees. He entered me with the same amount of energy he had while he was on top of me, but I knew I had his ass in this position.

One thing I have to say about the doggy-style, it's a win-win position, because if he knows what he's doing, you both come out on top.

He started pulling my hair and slapping me on my ass as I continued to back it on him harder and harder. I don't know what it was about me looking back at him, but the moment I did, we both exploded, loud and hard.

After a few moments of catching my breath, I looked up at the clock again and it read 12:42am.

"Dam, it's that late?" I asked him.

I couldn't have known what I was talking about, because the moment he looked up and saw what time it was, he jumped up.

"Dam, I still got a few things to take care of

227

before I fly out," he stressed as he led me to the bathroom.

After we showered, I warmed our food and we ate under candle light. I then gave him the few outfits and the Movado watch I'd bought him for his birthday. Before he walked out, he licked two of his fingers and eased them into my sore pussy.

"Deamon," I whined, "I'm sore."

He then took his fingers and placed them in his mouth before saying, "I just wanted to taste you before I left."

I grabbed his ass and practically threw my tongue down his throat. Being in love is hell, especially when you know that the one you're in love with can be snatched away from you at any moment.

-KRUGER-

Man, it's funny what a good sex session could do to a woman, not to mention what it could actually do to a man. As much as I hate to admit it, all that me and Teresa have right now is some great sex. And to keep it genuine, that sex shit just ain't enough for a playa.

It really ain't no secret, Teresa is a good woman. The thing is, she ain't for no street cat, her loyalty traits don't run deep enough. You know what though, I believe that she'll be the perfect woman for a square. Sometimes I really hate leaving her, but moving from her to Deidra, I ain't losing by a long shot.

Lord knows that I can't wait until we reach Miami tomorrow. Like Deidra told me earlier, we just need some fresh air.

My older cousin, Vito, suppose to meet us at the airport, he say that he has a present for me. That fool down there fucking with them Haitians, so I know that he's down there doing it big.

After riding around the city clearing my head, I found myself crawling in the bed next to Deidra.

"Hey baby-girl, how you doing?" I whispered as I pecked her on the back of her neck.

"A lot better with you right here," she replied as she turned around to face me.

"You miss me, huh?"

"I thought you said, what's understood doesn't need to be talked about?" She grinned.

"You know that I can't beat you like that," I

managed to reply.

"When it comes down to us, ain't nobody beating nobody, we gonna win this one together," she declared as she raised up and kissed me.

After releasing my tongue, she laid back down and said, "Now get some rest, we gotta leave here no later than 10:30, our flight leaves at one."

"Yes mamm," I replied.

"Deamon," she whispered after a few moments of silence.

"What's up baby-girl?"

"I love you."

I'm glad that she had her back to me, so she couldn't see the huge smile I was wearing, so I hit her with, "You done forgot already?"

"Forgot what?" She asked me.

"What's understood doesn't need to be talked about!"

****

"Baby, we're here," Deidra told me after she shook me awake.

My entourage consisted of seven couples. Burger and his baby mama Carla, Black and his shortie from Augusta State, Liz, Rip and his girl Stacy, Big Ox and this broad who went by the name Peaches, Slim and Vikki, Slanga and Amanda and me and Deidra.

I was so exhausted from the previous night, that Deidra had to literally bath me this morning. We were like two seconds from missing our flight all together, if it wasn't for her. I had already called Vito while we were driving to Atlanta, and he said that he'd meet us outside the terminal. After grabbing my bags, I spotted him and this female at the front entrance. After clearing the space between us, Vito gave me a huge bear huge, before introducing us all to his wife, Larissa.

"All of your rooms are paid for," he said.

"How much we owe you cuz-o?" I asked him.

He just looked at me as if I'd lost my mind, "Nothing, that's my present to you for your birthday."

Everyone thanked him for his generosity.

"Me and wifey have like three rental trucks outside to take ya'll to the hotel," he stated like a perfect tour guide, "so I need like two drivers to follow me."

"Dam cuz, I didn't know that you were a tour guide."

"I'm any and everything for blood cuz!" He replied then asked where my brother was.

"He got a baby on the way and mad bills to pay, so he had to work," I replied as I jumped in the Expedition with him.

Our rooms were on South Beach, so from the airport to the hotel, we talked about family. I guess you can say we sounded like two females with all the family gossip.

Larissa and Deidra hit it off from the beginning, they were already talking about certain spots they were gonna hit. I told Vito that I needed to get some rest, so he said he'd wake me up at nine. While all the fellas went to their rooms to lay it down for a minute, the females headed out with Larissa as their tour guide.

****

"So, what did you get Deamon for his birthday?" Larissa was asking Deidra as they

walked through Liberty Market.

"I haven't bought him nothing yet," Deidra confessed with a concerned expression before adding, "I was hoping to find him something down here."

Larissa and Deidra walked around together, while all the other girls were spread through-out the market.

"You know, every since Vito learned that Deamon coming down, I haven't heard nobody but him," Larissa revealed in that Haitian accent, "Deamon this, Deamon that."

Deidra giggled at the way that she talked before nodding her head in agreement and saying, "Deamon says that they're pretty close. But how long have ya'll been together?"

"Three years," she responded as she held up three fingers.

"So what did you get him for his last birthday?"

Larissa smiled as if the memory brighten her day before saying, "I spent 14 thousand on a Cuban link, charm and bracelet, and he never wears it."

"I think that's what I wanna get Deamon,

but if I do that, I want to get the charm custom made."

"My family will make that special for you. He works here. We put order in, and have it done Friday, hey?"

-KRUGER-

***"Say kinfolk*,"** I hear Vito yelling as he continued to bam on the room door, "is you ever coming out of there?"

"Ahh playboy, don't trip," I replied as I opened the door, "You was suppose to be here at nine, here it is 9:45."

"Oh yeah," he responded with a wide grin while grabbing his crotch, "something came up."

"I bet something did, but, where everybody else at?"

"From my understanding, something came up with them too, but they say they should be ready around ten."

"Well, we just jumped out the shower so give us until ten after," I replied.

"I feel you, but hurry up, cause Larissa

hungry," he disclosed before walking away.

Deidra had already put me on point on how all the woman had decided to come back here and seduce us, so I already knew that everyone would be behind schedule. By the time we reached the lobby, everybody was already there.

"About time, pretty boy," Slanga announced.

"Now, if anybody was gonna say anything, I knew it had to be you," I let him know.

"You dam right! Now let's go get something to eat," he stressed before we all walked out of the hotel.

After a twenty minute drive, we pulled in the parking-lot of a restaurant name Larissa's.

From the outside, Larissa's looked like all the other restaurant with the added extra tall palm trees in several locations near the entrance.

The inside was more exotic than anything. There were tropical fish aquariums located throughout the restaurant. It was semi-pack, but we had this special section in the back. The lights were dim, but they had candles on every table that gave it a romantic appeal. From the looks on every one of our faces, we all were digging it. After we all were seated, Larissa stood up.

"Welcome to Larissa's," she greeted us as if this was her favorite part, "we specialize in curry foods. Now I took liberty of ordering curry goat as main course, but if you like anything different, I will present to you."

She then looked over at Vito as if she was seeking his approval. He nodded his head with a smile, and she continued.

"By the way tonight's dinner is on me," she stated before looking over at me and adding, "sort of early birthday present, huh."

I smiled as I looked over at Vito, who just nodded his head with that smile again. Cuz-o has definitely out done himself with her. She's that female he always use to talk about having, when we was younger, so I'm happy that he's happy.

"I wanted a side order of that curry chicken and shrimp," Amanda blurted out.

"No problem," Larissa replied before asking, "anyone else?"

"Say cuz, lets step in the back for a minute," Vito implied as he raised from his seat, "please excuse us for a few," he said to everyone else.

My cousin has manners now, I never

thought I'd see the day. We walked in the back of the restaurant and stopped at a door labeled private.

After he knocked on the door a male voice from the other side said, "Come in."

Now whoever this cat was, he had his shit together. The first thing I remember seeing was all the surveillance monitors behind his desk. I could see dam near every part of the restaurant, including all my peoples at our table.

The office was decked out in glazed mahogany wood. Behind the desk sat an older black man with a devilish demeanor.

"What's going pop?" Vito greeted him.

"Just keeping an eye on things," he replied with a light smile exposing the fact that his entire bottom grill was gold.

"So this family, hey?" He asked.

"Yeah this him," Vito acknowledged as he looked over at me.

He asked with a suspicious expression, "What, he has no tongue?"

"Where I'm from sir," I stated after clearing my throat, "you only speak when you're spoken to."

STUCK

He just smiled before he replied, "He's your family alright."

"Vito has told me a lot about you. If ever in need, you shouldn't hesitate to come to us. Blood is thicker than water, and since Vito is connected to my blood-line, and you his, that makes me and you connected. And without a doubt Luther Wire takes care of his family."

"I preciate that Mr. Wire, I might soon take you up on that offer."

Man, Vito threw a major curve at a playa. I mean I knew he was in association with the Haitians, but I didn't know that his father in law was the Haitian version of Paulie from Goodfellas.

"The sooner the better," he turned back to his monitors, "I'm not gonna hold you from your guest, but make sure we talk again."

"No problem Mr. Wire," I stated as me and Vito turned to walk out.

By the time we made it back to the table everyone was tripping. After seeing all my peoples enjoying each other's company, I kind of felt bad about leaving Red and Pimp back home. So I told myself that I would check on them fools later.

When the food arrived, we was talking

about how all the girls came back from their outing and sexually harassed us.

"I didn't get any complaints when it was going down," Amanda stated with a look that let everyone know that she put it down.

"I know, right," Vikki added as she looked over at Slim.

"Ya'll know that they are gonna try to front for their homies," Carla stressed.

"I believe in letting them stunt, cause in the end I always get mine," Liz revealed.

"That's where I'm at too," Stacy agreed.

"So now what you got to say?" Ox looked over at his girl Tonya and asked.

"I really don't have to say anything!" She retorted, "The way you just reacted, said enough," she added causing everybody to burst out laughing.

"Now you ain't hear none of us say nothing, but you just had to open your mouth," Black stressed while trying to control his laughter.

By 12:30 we were tucking the girls in and headed for NW 27th Avenue to *Club RoleXX.*

When we stepped in the club, you could tell that cuz-o was a regular.

"Hey Vito, who are your cute friends?" The sexy red-bone asked who was playing the hostess role.

He introduced us all, and let her know that we came to have a good time.

"Well, you came to the right place Georgia boys, cause we're known for having good times," she stated with a seductive smile.

We had VIP off the chain as we gave every female in the club a chance to make some bread. We even took some photos to send to Hammah and Bad-Azz.

When I stepped in my hotel room later that night I went straight to the shower, because we all had that sex scent on us from the club.

The moment I cuddled up next to Deidra she asked, "Did you have fun?"

I kissed her on the cheek, "Yeah, but how you feeling?"

"I'm alright, I just missed you." She replied.

"Well, why you didn't call me?"

"You know that I'm not gonna harass you like that."

"I know, but let's get some rest."

"Alright, but can I get a good night kiss?" She asked with a sinister grin.

"See how you be trying to start?"

"What's wrong with that?" She questioned as she grabbed my dick.

After she felt that I was already hard, she smiled and asked, "How come you always say that you ain't ready, but he always say different?"

-TERESA-

Now what the hell is David writing Deamon for? Hell, how did he even get this address?

It's not like I was plundering or anything, but Ron left the letter on top of the microwave. I don't even suppose to be my ass over here like this, but I refuse to be the third leg in Ron and Toya's mission of playing house.

It's funny to me how me and Deamon introduced them and how their relationship blossomed from friends of friends, to dam near husband and wife in such a short time.

I ain't hating or nothing, but it gets to me at times, cause I really don't know what's the hold up with me and Deamon. It ain't like we haven't been trying. I may sound silly to some people, but what's so wrong with me wanting to have his baby.

I joked around with him about me getting pregnant the last time I talked to him on the phone, but we didn't talk long, because they were at the bowling alley, so I could hardly hear him. He called me back last night, but I was asleep, so I told him that I'd call him back, and of course I told him that I love him.

Sometimes I hate to even tell him that, because he never says it back. He's always saying some shit like, action speaks louder, like I don't never show him. Nigga please!

I try my best not to get in his business, and with the business that he's in, I really be wanting to stay away from his ass. But he really has me caught up.

I mean even when I'm mad at his ass, I can never stay for too long. All he has to do is look at me the wrong way, and I'm instantly wet. I love it when he baths me and gives me a massage right after, because he always seems to molest me in the process. But with all that in mind, I'm not so blind not to know that we really can't establish a future together with David meddling in our business.

242

****

"Surina, what the hell are you doing in there?" Her grandmother was asking after she knocked on the door.

"Nothing nana," she replied through the door.

"Well, you sure have been doing a lot of nothing lately. You know that I don't like you being in this room like this. Is there something you wanna talk to me about?"

"No mamm," Surina replied openly agitated, "I just have a lot on my mind."

"That boy ain't put his hands on you, did he?" She asked in a concerned manner.

"No mamm, I told you that I'm alright!" Surina declared with a little too much volume.

"Girl, open this dam door!" Her grandmother yelled, "It ain't no way that I'm talking through doors in my own house!"

Surina really didn't wanna open the door because she had been crying all day, and she definitely didn't want her grandmother to see her eyes all puffy. But she knew if she didn't open it, her grandmother was gonna kick the door in.

243

After opening the door her grandmother looked at her face and shook her head, "Now, what man got you in here crying your eyes out like this?"

"It's not just a man, nana, its Deidra too," Surina whined out as she wiped her eyes with the back of her hand.

"What happened girl?" She wrapped her arms around her.

"You remember Deamon?"

"That little black boy?" Her grandmother asked with a surprised expression.

"Yes mamm," she responded with a head nod, "him and Deidra suppose to be going together."

"And?" Her grandmother asked with a confused look before adding, "I thought that you didn't like him no more?"

Surina quickly pulled away from her grandmother and stared at her as if she'd lost her mind, "I never said that, I love him!"

Her grandmother just shook her head again, "It's not what you said, it's how you was acting. See, I remember when you use to get them letters from that boy and I remember reading some of those letters too. But the thing I can't remember is

244

you ever writing him back. Now, I know this is really none of my business, but in some of those letters that boy sounded as if you really disappointed him."

"And he still mad at me because I never wrote him," Surina sadly confessed with her chin in her chest.

She lifted Surina's head up, "If you truly love someone you never neglect them, regardless of the situation. Obviously, that boy thought ya'll was closer then you thought you were at the time. He was looking for you to be there for him, but all you did was turn your back on him."

"Now you know that I don't take sides in nothing, cause right is right and wrong is wrong," her grandmother continued, "but if you loved him like you're claiming now, you should've been there for him. But, what's done is done. It makes no since staying locked up in this room crying over no man. You're a beautiful young lady, you can practically get any man you want. Besides, what's wrong with that boy Jimmy?"

"Nothing, I just don't love him like I do Deamon."

Her grandmother just shook her head as she raised from the bed before saying, "Well, put some clothes on so we can spend some money, cause that's about the only thing that makes us smile at times like this."

"I can be ready in five minutes," she replied with a light smile.

Her grandmother just looked down at her and smiled, "Everything is going to work out how GOD wants it to, just repeat the serenity pray a few times, and you'll feel better."

Surina smiled as she watched her grandmother leave before she closed her eyes and said, "GOD, grant me the serenity to accept the things that I cannot change, courage to change the things that I can, and wisdom to know the difference!"

-KRUGER-

Here it is Friday night and we've been to dam near every strip club in Miami. What really caught my eye was Black Gold and Take One. I haven't been able to trick off any money, because the fellas ain't letting me go in pocket for nothing.

Even though all that clubbing is cool, it really ain't me, besides, I rather chill with Deidra. I really hate leaving her every night to spend money with broads I don't even know, I feel she deserves more than that. When I really look at it, I'm already working with a dime.

We just got back from swimming in the pool downstairs. Baby-girl was styling in this Gucci bathing suit that demanded everyone's attention. Amanda and Larissa had the same suit on, but Slanga and Vito couldn't help but have comments about my girl. Now when it's put out there like that, you know you're working with something.

This cat Luther is a pretty cool cat. He just hit me with a couple ounces of this hydro. At first that shit had a playa too high to even move. I was so zoned out, I was scared to add the *Hennessy* with it, but I'm kind of use to it now.

Teresa ole stalking ass is now staying at me and Ron's apartment. She obviously found a letter that her ex wrote me, because she asking all the crazy questions that I don't feel up to answering. I had to interrupt her interrogation and remind her that I'm trying to enjoy myself. That was just last night, so I'll be a fool to call her today. But knowing her, she'll call me in a while stressing about something else that she has no control over.

"Deamon, I hope you have that sliding door

opened?" Deidra is saying from the bathroom, "Between this steam and that smoke, I won't be able to see in here."

I walked over to her and picked her up while she was drying off.

"Deamon!" She yelled.

"Yeah, I got it open," as I carried her to the bed.

Man this woman is by far sexier fresh out the shower. I told her to turn over on her stomach as I grabbed the baby oil and a towel. After I finished drying her off, I began applying the baby oil on her back before I heard her sniffling.

"Dam, baby-girl, what's up with you?" I asked totally thrown by her reaction.

She turned around and faced me, and that's when I saw the tears streaming down her face, "You make me feel so special."

"Oh yeah," I replied, openly far from content with the mood.

She must have saw the confused expression on my face because she stressed, "I'm alright."

We both were silent for a moment before she asked, "Do you remember I use to get in all that trouble back in the day?"

"Yeah, I remember."

"Why do you think that I haven't been in any trouble lately?"

"You tell me."

"Because of you," she assured me as she turned on her side to face me, "if I get to acting foolish like I use to, you're not going to be dealing with me like you are now. That's the only real reason my daddy deals with this us thing, he knows you keep me straight."

I'm understanding where she's coming from, but I'm not understanding why she's bringing it up now.

"I just wanted you to know that I cherish every moment we spend together," she continued, "I never thought it was really ever possible that we'll be together like this. Look at you, you're a once in a lifetime type of man. I love the way you look, the way you talk and walk, but above all of that, I love the way you think."

"I mean if you're wrong, you're not ashamed to let it be known," she continued, "You're more than considerate when it comes down to us. I wish that we can stay here together, forever, because this week just isn't enough."

"I can definitely feel you on that. I mean all my people down here. The only one I would have to send for is Red."

"What about Pimp? I know you don't plan on leaving Pimp," she blurted out.

"Yeah, I guess you're right," I replied with a lack of contentment.

The first look that she gave me let me know that she was aware that I had doubt about Pimp, but her following expression let me know just how well she knew her position. See she knew that it wasn't in her best interest to question me on that, so she played the backfield on the subject. Gotta love her for that.

"Let's get up from here and take a walk on the beach or something," I finally said as I raised from the bed.

"I never thought you was the type to start something and not finish it!" She challenged with a sexy smile before pulling me back over her.

With no hesitation I passionately kissed her. Despite my sudden actions she was only a heartbeat away with her hands exploring my body. Before I knew it, I was completely naked with her reminding me just how good I do have it.

I don't know if it was her constant whimpering or her eagerness to meet my every stride, but she had my mind too far gone. But when I saw her tears, I knew that this was more than sex. We both had more emotions involved than I wish to admit. I wanted her to feel every inch of me, and I every spot in her. This wasn't just some good pussy, this was some good loving, and that's something us street cats don't feel too often. Moments later we both were letting out loud moans that scared the hell out of me.

"You alright baby-girl?" I asked after a few moments of staring at the ceiling in silence.

"Yeah, I'm alright," she assured with a sly grin as she rolled over on top of me, "It looks to me as if I need to be asking you that question."

I couldn't help but smile before I pulled her closer and buried my tongue in her mouth.

"You know that we ain't finish?" She stated after our lips separated.

I knew right then and there that it was gonna be a long night.

****

"Say Red," Pimp was saying, "have you heard from Black them?"

"Yeah, I talked to them yesterday, they might be back tomorrow."

They sat in the middle room of 1122 Summer Street playing chess. It was Sunday morning and the junkie traffic was still at a high speed. They had Butler at the door, so any sale that came through, he lead them to the middle room.

Butler had on the same clothes that he'd worn the day Kruger and the rest of the fellas left for Miami. He hadn't slept in the last three days, so when Vader came to the door he really wasn't as sharp as usual.

"Say Butler!" Red yelled from the middle room, "Who that out there?"

"This me, Vader!" He yelled back.

"Come on back," Red stressed.

When Vader stepped in the middle room, all he saw was smoke in the air, so he covered his face, "Ya'll stupid muthafuckas are on a one way trip to 401 Walton Way, Richmond County Jail!"

"What the hell is you talking about?!" Pimp demanded to know.

"Ya'll two fools lounging in this trap with all

this dope. To make shit worst, ya'll smoking weed like it's cool. And too top it all off ya'll got an even stupider muthafucka at the door!" He revealed as he took a seat on the couch before adding, "And the only reason he so stupid, is, he so scared that he's gonna miss his next hit that he can't even get no rest."

Red and Pimp burst out laughing while Vader pulled out his crack stem and a piece of wire hanger and started to push the remaining crack residue into the brillo he had stuffed in the stem.

"Ya'll laughing, but I'm serious!" He added, "Ya'll need to tell him to take his ass to bed and close up shop for the day. Or get ya'll ass out there and work that porch."

"Get your stupid ass off that couch!" Red yelled at him, "And put that dam stem back in your pocket cause you ain't about to smoke a muthafuckin thing in here!"

"What the fuck do you want anyway?" Pimp asked as Vader obeyed Red's command.

"I need a fifty," he replied.

"Go back to the front and I'll be up there in a minute," Pimp stressed.

"Hell na'll!" Vader retorted, "I wanna see

mine on the *Tanita* muthafucka!"

"On the what?" Pimp replied in a confused manner.

"The scale fool!" He disclosed, "I need to see my 1.5 on the scale, cause you the type to try and give a nigga a gram."

"Dam nigga, you don't trust me?" Pimp sarcastically asked.

"Fuck no!" Vader retorted, "This the game fool! And in the game you can't even trust your own mama. But you want me to break the codes and trust you?!"

"Nigga, just get to the door!" Pimp stressed as he shook his head in defeat, "I'll call you back in a minute."

On his way back to the front door Vader asked, "Did ya'll hear about somebody breaking in Kay-Kay's house and stealing Slanga's money?"

"What the fuck you say?!" Red retorted.

"Somebody broke in Kay-Kay's house and stole seven-five hundred," Vader replied.

"You bullshiting, when?" Pimp questioned.

"Just last night," Vader answered before adding, "Slanga gonna kill her ass. You know the first thing he gonna think is that she got it."

"You can come on back Vader," Pimp called.

"Boy, I'd really hate to be around when that fool gets back," Vader claimed as he walked back in the middle room.

"Whoever it was got them a nice lick," Pimp stressed.

"I don't think that Kay-Kay stupid enough to pull stunts like that," Red implied, "but a playa still can't put shit past these hoes."

"Who could be stupid enough to hit a nigga name Gunslanga?" Pimp asked in astonishment.

"I don't know what the hell you talking about, but any nigga can get it! The streets ain't got no love for nobody!" Red stressed.

"Here you go Vader," Pimp stated as he placed 1.3 on the scale.

"Now you must feel that I've fallen and can't get up, if you think you can handle me like that!" Vader stressed.

"Here man," Pimp stated openly aggravated as he dropped two tenths on the scale, "Now get the hell on!"

"If ya'll need me to watch the door for ya'll,

I'll do that, cause I would hate to see ya'll go out like that," Vader suggested.

"We straight," Red assured him.

"I'm down with ya homie!" he practically announced, "I mean, it's only two places that I ain't riding with ya, and that's the chain gang and the graveyard!"

"Where's that?" Red asked with a questionable expression.

"The chain- gang and the graveyard, playa!" He stated with a serious expression before adding, "Those are two places you gotta deal with solo."

They both burst out laughing as Vader made his way out the door. Only a few minutes had passed before Pimp realized that he never got his fifty Jugs.

"Dam, he got me for that 50!"He stated in a tone that said he was disgusted with himself.

"Dam nigga, how you slip like that?" Red asked, "You already know to be a point when he comes through."

"I know, but he'll be back," Pimp stressed.

"I doubt it, besides point seen, money lost," Red replied.

"I'll get it!" Pimp stated as if he was reassuring something.

"Man, dam them fifty bones, I need to call the fellas and let them know what's what with Kay-Kay," Red stressed as he grabbed his phone.

-KRUGER-

Besides a few people here and there, Miami Beach is pretty much deserted. Here it is 12:36, Sunday night, so maybe that's why. I stepped out by myself, just to marinate on this past week. I can't help but thank GOD for allowing me to be in this position. I mean look at me, I'm alive and free!

That nigga Slanga told me some helluva shit on my birthday. He stressed, "Nigga, you 21 and got more respect and clout than a fifty year old Baptist preacher." But to keep it genuine, I really can't see it.

Yesterday me, him and Vito drove to Ft. Myers to visit the rest of my family. Everyone acted as if they were happy to see us. Vito says he hardly goes home, because he don't want to put them in no unjust situation. For some reason he has the whole family thinking he's this long shore man on

STUCK

the port, man if they only knew.

While we were in Ft. Myers I got a chance to get up with my father. Well, let me rephrase that, my daddy. Because I feel that your father is someone who looks out for you, someone who takes care of you, someone you can look up too. I guess that's why people always say father figure. To me, your daddy just the cat your mama allowed to plant the seed.

I haven't seen or heard from him since I tried to live with him when I was younger, and that shit ain't work out at all. I had a little trouble in school and this dude figured whatever it was he could beat it out of me. I wasn't going for it, so I ended up moving back to Augusta with my mama.

When we met up, we embraced and all though, that's my daddy, ya heard. It wasn't like a family reunion or nothing like that, but I have to admit, it was good seeing him. Even though he hasn't been the person I felt he should've been to me, doesn't mean that I'm not gonna be who I am suppose to be to him. Two wrongs never made a right!

I remember when I was a jitt, I tried to run away to that fool on a bike. Picture my dumb ass riding up I-75 from Ft. Myers to Tampa, now that was some wild shit. I guess I was just feeling neglected by my mama them.

You know me and my step daddy ain't never was able to see eye to eye on nothing. I mean we was cool enough to get through like 13 or 14 years together though. He just had too many other things going on to really tune in to what I had going on.

I guess you can say that my hate for them comes from the way they treated me when I was locked up. Every now and then I'll call home and my so-called family wouldn't even accept my calls. It's funny to me now, because I realize that neither of us was given a script on the way we suppose to handle certain situations. Most of us just doing the best we can.

Besides, we have the same blood running through our veins, so I could never play them to the left. I just wish they would think like I think sometimes, but on that aspect I'm just a dreamer.

Hell, since yesterday I've been in this storm for 21 years, so if I haven't learned how to deal with it by now, I might as well call the grim reaper myself.

But you know, now that I've experienced a few things in life, I realize that it wasn't my mama them fault that they were too young to know how to raise a playa. To keep it genuine, I'm kind of glad that I've been through what I've been through, because all of my trials have molded me into this character they see daily.

"Smile For Me Now!" I screamed out toward the water, feeling 2-Pac and Scarface to the fullest.

We should be back in Augusta no later than tomorrow night. You would think that we would hit the Garden City and get back to getting this money, but we already have to see about a dummy.

As one might say, we have a little lesson to teach the streets of Augusta, because when you snatch from my brother's plate, you're snatching from mine. Nino and G-Money was actors searching for Oscars, but I'm sincerely my brother's keeper! I guess I'll be putting them twin Colt .45's, that Vito bought me for my birthday, to use sooner than I thought.

Besides the twins, everything else I received was jewelry and clothes. Even Luther hooked me up with a nice diamond infested pinky ring. But out of all the gifts, Deidra took the cake with the Summer Street medallion. But when it all boils down, I can't enjoy none of it, I gotta help my nigga deal with this thing that's going down with his side team.

****

Kay-Kay sat on the couch inside of Gunslanga's trap house on Summer Street. Her and Prime had been up all night trying to figure out who broke in her apartment.

Prime was in the backyard feeding the four pit-bulls. He really was wishing that he could get away until all the drama blew over, but Gunslanga gave him specific instructions not to go anywhere.

"I don't know why he wants me here?" Prime asked as he walked in through the back door.

"You know how your cousin is," Kay-Kay replied with her eyes glued on DMX and Nas in the movie Belly on the big screen.

"Girl you sitting up in here watching that bullshit like everything all good," he stated as he glared at her from the kitchen, "but Slanga gonna beat your ass."

"Whatever," she rebutted as she waved him off, "I didn't do nothing and you know it."

"How the fuck is I'm suppose to know?" He quizzed her.

"Cause we been together the whole time they been gone," she explained with a blank expression.

"Now if you tell that fool that, he gonna think that we're fucking, and we both hit him for that bread."

"You think that's what he thinking?" She inquired with a questionable expression.

"You mean to tell me that you done told him that already?" He asked in disbelief.

"Yeah, it's the truth ain't it?!" She retorted.

"Stupid bitch!!" He yelled as he walked in the front room where she was, "You done put me in the middle of this bullshit! Now that nigga don't wanna hear nothing, but where his money at. I can't believe that your ass is that slow!"

"What else was I suppose to tell him?" She asked with a sad face.

"You could have told that fool anything, but you was with me! Now I'm subject to catch a slug behind something that I ain't have nothing to do with."

"He ain't gonna do nothing to you, ole scary

ass nigga, you his cousin!" She stressed.

"Bitch, shut the fuck up! Your ass don't know shit!" He walked back towards the kitchen, "If he feels that we got him for that cheese, than we dead, point-blank period! That nigga could care-less about us being blood."

Kay-Kay watched as Prime walked out the back door, before she turned her attention back to the big screen. She wasn't really watching DMX act a fool in the basement by making that guy get Jug naked, in her mind, that was Gunslanga doing that to her and Prime.

****

"So what's going?" Kruger was asking Gunslanga.

They were riding in Gunslanga's Lincoln as *Twista's*, 'Adrenaline Rush', hummed through the sound system.

"I really can't call it right now," Gunslanga paused for a minute, "but as soon as we shake a few trees, something is bound to pop out."

"You got anybody in mind?" Kruger asked him.

263

STUCK

"Yeah, it's these cats I've been serving who grinding right down the street. They the only ones that I know really know that shit really be there. I fucked up when I let her serve them."

Kruger saw the look of regret on his comrade's face, "So how you wanna handle it?"

"Let's check out the crib and then go from there."

After pulling in front of the apartment building, Kruger jumped out and went straight to the trunk and grabbed his chrome twins. The moment they both walked up the stairs to the apartment, they noticed that her door was clear off the hinges.

"Playboy, we ain't gotta go in there cause that door was definitely kicked in," Kruger pointed out before he placed the twins in the seam of his jeans and throwing his shirt over them.

Gunslanga knocked on the neighbor's door. They could here that someone was watching re-runs of In Living Color. A few moments later, an older woman opened the door.

"Yes, can I help you?" She asked with a flower printed night gown on and pink hair rollers in her head.

"Yes mamm," Gunslanga replied, "our sister stays in the apartment that was broken in the other night and we just wanted to know if you saw anything."

"I've told her over and over how them boys from down the street was walking past here more than usual, but she doesn't pay me no mind." She stated, "See, I live alone, and I be scared that they'll eventually come and try to do something to me, so I be watching."

"You're right, I can't understand, why people invade other folks privacy like that," Gunslanga agreed.

Kruger just looked over at his comrade and shook his head, "I apologize Miss, but we have to be going."

"How is she, is she alright?" She asked in a concerned manner.

"She's fine and thanks for asking," he replied before following Kruger down the stairs.

They walked six houses down the sidewalk where two guys were sitting on the porch.

"Say fellas," Gunslanga called out.

They looked up but never replied.

"Say playboy," Kruger stated, "ya'll ain't

hear my people talking to ya'll?"

The bigger of the two stood up and said, "What's going Slanga?"

"I thought that ya'll would be able to tell me," Gunslanga calmly replied.

"What you mean?" The guy responded in a dumbfounded manner, "Tell you what?"

"Playboy, fuck this here," Kruger stressed as he jumped the fence, "Ya'll niggas think that we walked all the way down here to play guessing games? One of ya'll niggas know who broke in that house down there!" As he walked up to the bigger of the two.

"Man we ain't have nothing to do with that," the bigger of the two practically whined out before Gunslanga jumped the fence.

That's when the little guy tried to run past Gunslanga, but Gunslanga clothe-lined him hard to the ground.

"Now ya'll about to piss a nigga off!" Gunslanga stressed, "If you ain't did shit, what you trying to run for?"

The little guy was still on the ground with his hands around his neck when his friend stated, "He ain't have nothing to do with that, the nigga ya'll looking for is Jug."

That's when Kruger pulled one of the twins from his waist and slapped him across the face with it. The guy instantly fell to the ground with blood spitting out of his left cheek.

"The next time we come through here asking about something, don't give a playa the run around!" Kruger stated while standing over the guy, "See we could've looked out for ya'll, but instead you forced a playa to handle shit this way ," he walked away and jumped back over the fence.

"If ya'll see that nigga Jug, tell him to find me before I find him," Gunslanga stressed before following Kruger.

When they were back in the Lincoln headed for Summer Street Gunslanga asked, "Why did you hit dude after he told us what we wanted to know?"

"Three simple reasons playboy," Kruger replied with a sly grin, "One, for not giving it to us off top. Two, is I grabbed the twins out the trunk, so I had to use them in some way. And number three, bra, you had done clothes lined buddy so hard, I just had to try and top that."

His last reason caused them both to burst out laughing. They rode the rest of the way listening to Twista. When they reached Summer St., Kruger dropped Gunslanga off in front of his trap house and drove down and parked in front of 1122.

All of the fellas were on the porch giving Red and Pimp the highlights of the week, as he stepped out of the Lincoln.

"So where are these twins these niggas keep screaming about?" Red asked him as he climbed the stairs and sat next to him.

"They in the trunk, I'll let you peep them a little later," Kruger replied.

"They say we missed some real shit," Red stressed.

"Yeah, it was mad love."

"I heard about this off the wall Summer Street necklace," Pimp stressed, "pull it out."

"It ain't time yet," he replied with a wider grin, "but I'll pull it out Friday, along with a few other things."

"Say Kruger," Rip stated, "I need to holler at you when you get a chance."

"Waiting on you big homie," he raised up and headed down the sidewalk towards Gunslanga's trap.

"My nigga, I'm hurting," Rip stressed as he caught up with him, "I had six ounces stashed in the back, but somebody done hit me up. To top it off, I only got like 1,600 to bounce back on."

"Dam," Kruger stressed as if he himself took the lost, "you trying to grind tonight?"

"Dam right! I gotta bounce back like yesterday."

"I can feel that," he stated with a mutual understanding as he grabbed his phone and dialed the familiar digits.

"Hello," Deidra answered.

"You sleep?"

"No, I've been waiting for you to call."

"I need you right fast."

"How many?"

"How you know?"

"This me boo, give your girl some credit."

"My bad," he replied with a slight grin as he looked over at Rip, "bring me two boo."

"Do you want me to bring them, or are you coming to get them?" She asked.

"Bring them, cause I'm gonna leave with you."

"Give me thirty minutes!"

"Ole girl about to bring you a quarter, so just shoot me 4,500. You should be able to cook no less than thirteen, after that, it's all on you."

"That's what's up!" Rip replied with a huge grin.

As they approached Gunslanga's house they could hear him yelling. When they finally knocked on the door, he even yelled at them.

"Who the hell is it?!"

"This Rip and Kruger," Rip replied.

Prime opened the door with a look as if he was glad that someone had interrupted whatever was going on.

"Dam playboy, I can hear you all the way in the street, what up?" Kruger questioned.

"These muthafuckas still don't know nothing!" He retorted, "For all I know, they got my money and they trying to play me with this burglary shit!"

"Let me holler at you outside for a minute," Kruger insisted.

"Rip, make sure these two muthafuckas don't move!" Gunslanga stated as he made his way out the door.

Kay-Kay and Prime gave Kruger a look as if their future was now in his hands.

"Yeah, what up?" Gunslanga asked after they were outside.

"Man, what the hell is you doing?" Kruger questioned.

"Playboy, I'm securing my cheese," he responded with a sly grin, "if this nigga Jug skips town or something, I have to make them feel responsible."

"So what Prime had to do with it?"

"Nothing really," he chuckled out, "but for some reason he feels he do, and I ain't the type of cat to be changing his way of thinking."

"True."

"Either way it go, I'm getting my money back."

"I can respect that," Kruger replied after understanding the logic, "anyway, I'm about to ride out, so here is the keys to the Lincoln. Just remember them twins are in the trunk."

"I gotcha playboy."

"Rip, lets ride big homie," Kruger yelled out.

STUCK

Rip stepped out and him and Kruger made their way back towards 1122, leaving Gunslanga with his crew.

****

"I thought that you were suppose to be back last night?" Teresa was questioning Kruger.

It was 10:40am and he'd just woke her up with a kiss on her forehead.

"I see you're just making yourself at home," he replied as he sat next to her on the bed.

She gave him a devilish look that told him that wasn't the answer she was looking for.

"Now what's that for?" He asked her.

"I cooked your black ass a roast and everything," she revealed in a disgusted manner.

"I'll just eat it for breakfast," he replied while laying on top of her.

She pushed him off of her and stated, "Nigga, I didn't cook it for breakfast, I cooked it for dinner, last night!"

"I tell you what," he stated with a light grin, "you're off for the next three days, right?"

"So," she replied with a light smile.

"So we can do whatever you want."

"It's not like that Deamon!" She stressed in an aggravated manner, "All I want is for us to spend some time together."

"Ahh, ain't that sweet," he chuckled while squeezing her thigh.

"See, why you playing like that," she asked in a childish manner.

"Stop tripping. I haven't seen you in a week and this is how you wanna act."

"Man, I'm about to go," she stated while raising up to head to the bathroom.

He pulled her back to him and buried his tongue in her mouth. Despite her hard demeanor, she had really missed him and the way she responded to his kiss let him know just how much.

When they finally separated he asked her, "So how was your week?"

"It was alright, but I really missed you," she replied with her piercing green eyes.

"Well, I'm here now. So what were you planning on doing with me?" He challenged after he laid her on her back.

273

"That's why I really don't like you," she stated with a sly grin of her own.

"Why you don't like me?"

"Would you just shut up and kiss me again!"

After a few moments of foreplay, she jumped up and stressed, "I got a hair appointment with Tina at 11:30."

His demeanor showed that he wasn't feeling her cutting him off like that, but he kept his composure and asked, "What, you need some money or something?"

Despite the words that came out of his mouth, she noticed his uneasiness behind her actions, but she paid him no mind. To her, this was payback.

"No, I don't need any right now, but I do need you to meet me here around four," she replied as she threw on a pair of shorts and a white t-shirt.

"Make sure you brush your teeth," he informed with a light smile.

"You trying to say my breath stink?"

"I mean, you did just wake up didn't you?"

"Well, why you put your tongue all in my

mouth?"

"Cause I can do that," he replied as headed to the kitchen.

"I'm taking your car because it rides smoother than mine," she said after coming out of the bathroom.

"I thought it was too long and ugly."

"That's how I felt before I got behind the wheel," she confessed before kissing him and walking out.

When he looked around the apartment he realized that she had practically moved in. Her boots were in the middle of the floor and her uniform was thrown all over the sofa. The entire apartment had this feminine appeal to it. He wanted to call Ron and ask him what he was thinking about, but he knew that he would only be wasting his breath.

"Now this just some more shit I gotta deal with," he said to himself, "I can't believe that she done bomb rushed a playa's pad like this."

Just when he said that, his phone rang.

"Yeah," he answered.

"Youngblood, what's going?" Firebug replied.

"What up old man?"

"I guess I ain't good enough to hear from you on your birthday," he complained.

"Why you ain't just call the phone?" Kruger questioned.

"I did, ain't nobody answered though."

"You be calling from these blocked numbers and you know I ain't too funny gonna answer them like that."

"I'll go for that this time," he chuckled, "but have ya'll got things back on schedule?"

"Yeah, somewhat, but how the rest of that info coming?"

"We still working on it, but its coming. What, they harassing ya'll again?"

"Not that I know of, but as soon as we get that we can make some kind of move."

"I can dig that, but where Slanga at?"

"He around, hit his phone, he should answer."

"I guess I'll see you in a few days."

"Alright, be safe pop."

"You do the same," Firebug replied before he hung up.

276

(CHAPTER 9)

"Say Weasel," Jimmy stated from the passenger seat as they were riding with the top down, listening to UGK's, 'Riding Dirty', and smoking on a blunt, "did you see the truck ole boy brought out?

"Na'll, what color is it?" Weasel asked.

"Man, its money green and it's sitting on some major chrome!" Jimmy replied causing Weasel to turn the convertible around and head for Summer Street.

The truck was parked in Gurley's parking lot, so Weasel parked right next to it. They both hopped out the car and started appraising the Tahoe.

The paint was so glossy that it looked like a wet jolly rancher. The interior was laced with buckskin with the wood grain trimmings all throughout it. They noticed a 16 inch flip-screen television in the ceiling for the passengers, and one attached on the disc player.

"Dam, ya'll must be looking to get ya'll

heads took off!" The familiar voice stressed from behind them.

Weasel turned around and saw Kruger standing there holding an orange juice before he replied with, "Nigga, you done tricked the entire game with this here Hoe."

"Oh yeah," Kruger replied with a sly grin before adding, "what's understood don't need to be talked about."

"Yeah, yeah, yeah," Weasel replied, "just let a nigga hear what the system sounds like."

Kruger looked over at Jimmy and could tell that he felt out of place, so he told them both to get in.

"Ya'll don't have no where ya'll have to be, do you?" He asked after they all settled in.

"Na'll playboy we straight," Weasel answered for the both of them before looking back at Jimmy and implying, "Jim-bo, lets switch seats.

"Nigga, why you wanna switch seats?" He questioned with a confused expression.

"Cause I wanna see what movie this nigga got in here."

While Weasel moved to the back and Jimmy moved to the passenger seat, Kruger was tampering with his disc player. A few moments later the sounds of *Scarface's*, 'My Homies', blasted through the speakers.

As they rode around, the movie Scarface was playing on the screen, and by the look on Weasel's face he was loving every minute of the event. When Kruger sparked up a blunt, he practically put both of his passengers to sleep. When he realized that they were moments away of becoming his responsibility, he drove back to Summer Street.

All three of them got out of the truck and started walking towards the boarding house. Before they could reach the porch, Butler greeted them with some disturbing news.

"They just took Red, Black, Rip and Burger to jail for smoking on the porch."

Kruger just shook his head, grabbed his phone and dialed the familiar digits.

"Hello," Deidra answered.

"What up baby-girl?"

"Hey baby, what's up?"

"I need you to call 401 and see how much the bond is for Jay Grey, Bill Bryant, Joseph Cabbage and Nick Anderson is."

279

"Alright boo, I'll call you right back," she replied right before the line went dead.

"Dam playboy, I'm digging the way you handled that there," Weasel revealed with a smile of approval.

"It ain't nothing changed on this side, bra!" Kruger assured him with a smile of his own before noticing that Butler was still a little shook, "Everything all good Butler, they'll be out in a minute."

"I just hate that it happened," Butler stressed, "all they have to do is listen sometimes. You need to talk to them, because they'll listen to you."

Kruger just gave him a sly grin before stressing, "Man, I'm the young Jug, and they ain't too funny trying to hear what the young Jug gotta say."

"They'll listen, you just ain't tried yet," Butler assured him as Kruger's phone started ringing.

"Yeah, what up baby-girl?"

"They already bonded out," Deidra stated through the receiver.

"All of them?"

"Yeah, my friend in booking said that they all had money in their pocket."

"Well, I'm about to scoop them up."

"Baby, make sure you tell Red that my friend in booking wants to take him out," Deidra added.

"Oh yeah?"

"Uh huh, she said that he was cute."

"I'll make sure I tell him."

"Am I gonna see you tonight?"

"Yeah, if that's what you really want."

"Alright, I'll talk to you later."

"Now you know that you need to be ready to do more than that," he implied before hanging up the phone.

Kruger jumped back in his truck as Weasel and Jimmy pulled off headed towards the county. They offered to follow him, but he declined. It seem as if the moment he pulled in the parking lot, his comrades were making their way out the door.

"Dam bra, your timing couldn't be better," Hamburger hopped in the passenger seat while the rest of them piled in the back.

"Man, what happened?" Kruger

questioned.

"Them folks just caught a nigga smoking," Black replied, "and you know ain't nobody claimed the blunt, so we all went down."

"So, who blunt was it?" Kruger pried.

"It was all of our blunt!" Rip replied.

"Bra I ain't investigating ya'll or no shit like that," Kruger assured, " I'm just saying, the next time one of ya'll needs to claim it, so that all of ya'll won't get locked up, common sense!"

"You right, but you know that a nigga ain't trying to put claim to nothing!" Hamburger argued.

"Yeah, but if I was on the porch I'll probably still be in the holding cell with a parole hold," Kruger stressed.

"You right," Hamburger finally agreed, "that's why I was in such a rush to get out, because you know me, Red and Black already on probation for the same shit."

"My bad then," Rip stressed, "the next time I'll just claim it."

"Man fuck that," Hamburger stressed, "take me by Burger King before we head back to the Summer."

Kruger then passed his sack and a box of blunts to Rip before saying, "Say Red."

"Yeah, what up?" Red replied.

"It seems that you raised some hell in booking, ole girl told Deidra that she wanna holler at you."

"Oh yeah?" Red smiled.

"Yeah, I'm just passing the message playboy," Kruger replied with a smile of his own before turning the music back up.

****

It was a peaceful night at 1122 Summer Street as Red, Rip, Georgia Slim and Big Ox sat on the porch. Kruger was in the front room resting, while Hamburger and Black was in the middle room playing chess when the rusty colored box Chevy pulled in the front of the boarding house with Gunslanga on the passenger side.

"What up Slanga?" Big Ox greeted him as he made his way out the car and up the steps with the driver right behind him.

"What up playboy, I need to use ya'll scale

for a minute," he replied.

"You know where it's at," Rip replied.

"In the kitchen, right?"

"Yeah, the first drawer by the sink."

"Where everybody at?" He asked as he walked in the house.

"Kruger in that first room laying down and Burger and Black in the middle room," Big Ox replied.

Gunslanga walked in the first room where Kruger was and tapped his feet, "Playboy, it's about to go down."

"Man, didn't you learn when you was locked up that you don't wake a playa up while he resting! That's the most peaceful time of the day."

"Come on fool! Fuck you doing resting in here for anyway!" Gunslanga stressed.

Kruger got up and followed Gunslanga and the guy down the hall and in the kitchen. Once they entered the kitchen Gunslanga turned around and slapped the guy across the face with a pistol. The guy immediately fell to the ground holding his face and screaming. All the fellas heard the unfamiliar thud and the screaming and rushed to the kitchen.

Kruger looked up at Gunslanga with a puzzled expression and asked, "What up?"

"Man, this that nigga Jug!" He angrily responded before kicking the guy in the face and adding, "This brave muthafucka finds me and say he wanna buy two ounces. He done bought this bullshit ass Eddie gold and that raggedy ass Chevy out there with my bread!"

Hamburger rushed to the front to lock the house up. When he reached the door, Vader was walking on the porch and heard the guy screaming for help, so Hamburger pulled him in.

"What's up Burger?" Vader asked nervously.

"Shut the fuck up and stay right here!" Hamburger responded while grabbing the two by four from the door and heading back to the kitchen.

The moment Hamburger stepped one foot in the kitchen he started beating the guy across the head with the board while asking, "Where the fuck that money at?!"

Vader stood frozen at the door scared to death. From where he stood, all he could see was Hamburger cocking the board back to hit his target. And all he heard was a loud thud and a scream

285

every time Hamburger hit his target.

Kruger stepped in front of Hamburger and told the guy to strip. After grabbing the car keys from his pants pocket, he walked outside to the rusted colored Chevy and drove it in the backyard. After backing it in towards the back door, he popped the trunk and pulled the huge car speakers out and placed them in the backseat.

When he went back in the house he opened the back door. By that time this guy Jug stood in the middle of the kitchen butt ass naked, and Vader had finally built up enough nerve to ease down the hall to get a clearer view.

"You know you're about to take me to get the rest of my money, right?" Gunslanga was saying to his bloody victim.

This guy Jug just nodded as if he was a child. The moment Vader got a full view of the bloody victim he fainted.

"I got it from here fellas," Gunslanga stated after his victim was secured in the trunk of the Chevy.

"You sure you don't want me to ride with you playboy?" Kruger questioned.

"Na'll homie, I wanna deal with this one

dolo," he assured with a devilish grin.

"I can feel that," Kruger claimed with a little uneasiness, "just hit me up and let me know what the business is."

"Just keep your phone on," he responded right before he jumped in the driver's seat and pulled off.

When they all finally walked back in the house, they noticed that the floor was full of blood and Vader was still knocked out on the floor in the hallway. So Red got a jug of water and threw it on Vader. He woke up as if he was drowning while Kruger stood over him.

"Now its one or two things we can do with you," Kruger pointed out.

Vader's eyes were now as big as golf balls as he nodded his head.

"Now we can either take you through the same thing buddy just went through, or you can clean this mess up and keep your mouth shut."

Vader just nodded his head again.

"So which one is it's gonna be?" Hamburger asked while standing next to Kruger with the bloody two by four in hand.

****

"Deamon, wake up," Deidra was saying as she shook him awoke.

Right before he went to sleep Kruger had told her to watch his phone for a call from Gunslanga, so after seeing that it was him calling, she answered it.

"Yeah," Kruger finally stressed through the receiver.

"Where you at?"

"Homewood Suites."

"What room?"

Kruger looked over at Deidra and asked, "What room is this?"

"320," she replied as she was doing her hair.

"320, playboy," he stressed through the receiver as he sat up.

"I'll be there in like thirty minutes," Kruger heard before the line went dead.

"What time is it?" He asked her after realizing that she was fully dressed.

"It's almost 9:30," she replied as she sat next to him in the bed.

"What time do you have to be at work?" He asked as he massaged the back of her neck.

"Ten," she moaned.

"Let me stop rubbing on you, cause you'll never go to work and I'll never open the door for Slanga when he get here," is what he confessed right before he kissed her on the forehead.

Kruger stared at her for a moment and couldn't help but notice the disturbed expression she wore on her face so he stressed, "Don't worry about me baby-girl, I'll be careful out here."

She just smiled and said, "You think you know me, don't you?"

"You saying I don't?" He crossed-examined with a sly grin.

She then leaned over and pecked him on the lips before saying, "I'll see you when I get off."

Five minutes later she was pulling out of the parking lot and he was in the shower. He was just getting out of the shower when Gunslanga knocked on the door, so he ended up opening the door with a towel wrapped around him.

"Man, if you don't go and put some clothes

on," Gunslanga stressed as he walked in the room, "I done seen enough naked men for one lifetime."

"I can feel you on that," Kruger agreed with a sly grin before asking, "but is everything - everything?"

"Yeah and no," he nervously replied as he took a seat on the couch.

"So what up?"

"I got most of my bread back, but I had to take that nigga to the hospital."

"What?!" Kruger retorted.

"Yeah," Gunslanga replied as he nodded his head, "we was riding down East Bound and somehow the nigga pop the trunk from the inside and jumped out. He ended up running to the Smile Gas on the corner of Laney-Walker and East Bound. I had to jump out and yoke him back to the car, but the lady in the store saw me snatch his ass up. So that alone stopped his death sentence."

Kruger just stood there for a moment in silence allowing what he was just told to marinate before he finally asked, "You don't think the fool gonna tell the police who did it?"

"You never know," he replied in a sadden tone before adding, "but it's gonna be hard to explain to the police how I tortured him and then took him to the hospital."

Kruger just shook his head in disbelief before asking, "What car you in?"

"The Lincoln."

"Well, I'm gonna get this room for another day, so you can chill here until I find out what's going," Kruger stated before adding, "give me the keys to the Lincoln and you take the truck, just in case you have to dip."

"That's what's up, because I'm tired as a hell anyway," he replied as if he was totally exhausted.

"I'll bring the twins up here too, just in case," Kruger stressed, "and don't get on the messed up bed," he added with a sly grin.

✳✳✳✳✳✳✳✳✳✳✳✳✳✳✳

Vader stood at the steel security gate of 1122 directing the fiend traffic, while all the fellas were in the middle room playing *NBA Live* on the *Playstation*. It had taken Vader over two hours to clean all the blood from out of the kitchen and the hallway. After cleaning everything else in the house, the fellas didn't feel right just letting him walk away. They knew they couldn't take the chance of him going to the police, and since Butler was gone for a few days, they put him in charge of the door until everything cooled down.

The way the fellas looked at it, the best way to keep him cool was to keep him high, so they all went to their stashes and broke him off. So by the time Kruger stepped in the house, Vader's spirits were lifted.

"What up Vader, you alright?" Kruger quizzed.

"Yeah, I'm alright, but I still have to holler at you," Vader replied while pulling him in the first room.

"What up?"

"You know me and you alright, so I feel that I can holler at you," Vader declared with a disturbed expression.

Kruger just nodded his head.

"You have to know that the folks are subject to ride through here after what happened last night, don't you?"

"Yeah, and?" He replied with another head nod.

"So go and tell them stupid muthafuckas in there to get that dope out of this house!" Vader stated before adding, "The only muthafucka who should have dope in here is me, because I'll eat mine if I have to!"

"Alright," Kruger stressed as he turn to go and holler at the fellas.

"Hold up!" Vader stressed with a sly grin as he stood in front of the doorway, "Now, I done cleaned up everything, so you know you owe me."

"Yeah, I got you, just give me a minute," he stressed as he walked past him and up the hall.

"What up fellas?" He greeted as he stepped in the middle room.

After scouting the room, the first thing he noticed was that everyone was there but Black and Big Ox.

Pimp looked up and paused the game before stressing, "Nigga, ya'll crazy as hell! Where that nigga Slanga at anyway?"

"I can't tell you playboy, I haven't seen him since last night," Kruger replied, a little bewildered on where Pimp was coming from.

"You know after all the work the Summer put in, that nigga Slanga got all the glory from last night," Pimp implied.

"Nigga, what the hell is you talking about?!" Kruger questioned.

"I'm talking about them folks ain't looking for nobody but Slanga!" He stated in a disgusted manner, "They got his name ranging over the city like he John Gotti or something."

"Dam my nigga," Kruger spat out, "it sounds like you doing a little hating or something real close to it."

"Nigga, you should be happy that none of our names came up!" Red pressured.

"Don't get it twisted fool, I'm good!" Pimp assured, "I was knee deep in some good ass pussy last night when the shit went down."

Kruger just shook his head in disgust before asking, "Ain't nobody dirty is it?"

"Yeah, why, what's up?" Pimp admitted.

"What the hell you mean what's up?!" Kruger retorted, "Ain't you the same nigga who say them folks riding looking for Slanga? Where the hell do you think the crime scene is?" He added before he walked out the room and out the front door.

Vader ran behind him calling his name.

"What up Vader?" He asked after stopping in the middle of the street.

"Listen man, you have to do something about them stupid muthafuckas in there, especially that nigga Pimp."

"What you talking about now?" Kruger challenged.

"That nigga Pimp act as if ya'll owe him something."

"Say Vader," Kruger interrupted, "before you say anything, I can feel where you're coming from, but you know that you're out of pocket. With you being in the game, despite your smoking habit, you know your position, so I advise you to play it."

Vader just shook his head and stressed, "Just be careful."

Kruger walked towards Gunslanga's house without another word spoken. When he made it to the house, he knocked on the door and Kay- Kay appeared.

"What's going, and where Prime at?" He asked as he walked in.

"He went to get something to eat last night and never came back," she replied with a sly grin.

"You off in here by yourself?"

"Yeah, and I was getting kind of lonely too," she replied with a sexy smile.

"Well, we can deal with that later, right now I have something else that I have to tend to," he revealed with a gruesome expression.

"What's up," she stuttered out, "is everything alright?"

"Shit could always be better," he replied before asking, "you heard from Slanga?"

"Na'll, but they say them folks looking for him," she notified.

"Yeah, I heard, but do you got enough to hold you down for a minute?"

"The little bit I do got, I should be through with it by tonight," she claimed as she took a seat on the couch.

"Well you know my number, so when you get down to your last hit me up," he implied as he walked toward the door.

"Call me if you need me for anything," is how she extended her hand as she rose from the couch.

"You be safe and make sure you don't keep that work in here, cause them folks subject to come through here looking for Slanga," he pointed out as he walked out the door headed toward Dyess Park.

When he finally reached the Lincoln in the parking-lot, he sat in the car for a moment before cranking it. He then turned on the disc player and slid in *8-Ball and MJG's*, 'On Top Of The World', album.

He then grabbed a Swisher from the ashtray and slit it down the middle with his finger nails. After opening the car door, he dumped the contents of the blunt in the parking-lot. He then grabbed the bag of hydro from the glove compartment, and filled the leaf up with the weed. After rolling it and drying it with the lighter, he fired it up and took a deep puff. After skipping the disc to track four he sat back and enjoyed the music.

(CHAPTER 10)

Georgia Slim and Black sat on the porch of 1122 while Vader stood behind the security gate. It had been a little over 48 hours since the beat down in the kitchen, and they both were in awe of the fact the police hadn't come to investigate yet.

"I don't know why Slanga ain't take buddy head off and been done with it!" Black was stressing with a look of frustration.

"You know they say the broad at the store saw him yank ole boy up, so he probably would have a murder case instead of aggravated assault and kidnapping," Georgia Slim reasoned.

"My nigga, the way them folks throwing out that time, it wouldn't even matter," Black stressed before adding, "hell, you see what they did to Hammah."

"You might be right, but if you think about it, shit really ain't as bad as it look," Georgia Slim implied, "Slanga can probably pay his way out of this one."

"Yeah, but check this, how much would you charge me for beating you and putting you in your own trunk Jug-naked?" Black quizzed causing them both to burst out laughing.

"Dam," Vader interjected from behind the gate, "I gotta get away from ya'll fools. Ya'll muthafuckas crazy! I mean ya'll actually think that shits funny!"

"Shut the fuck up nigga!" Black blasted, "Your ass think it's funny when you be around here creeping niggas bombs, so I think it's funny when it catch up with you!"

"You ain't gonna think it's funny when them folks pull up and take your gorilla looking ass to jail for smoking weed on that dam porch again," Vader stressed before adding, "now laugh at that muthafucka!"

"Vader," Black called out in a humble manner, "I think it's best for you to find something safe to do."

After seeing that Black was serious, Vader stepped away from the gate and walked in the first room.

"Muthafucka!" Vader yelled out, "I got

away from the door so that you can calm down,
but just as soon as we get back on good terms, I'll
be right back at that fucking gate!"

"Man, he stupid as hell," Georgia Slim
stated while attempting to hold back from
laughing.

"Man, dam Vader," Black stressed as he
looked down the sidewalk, "who the hell is that
walking down this way?"

"Playboy that's Kay-Kay," Georgia Slim
replied with a light smile, "she looking right too."

Kay-Kay sashayed down the sidewalk as if
she was modeling for Girbuad. She wore a pair of
khaki capri's and a white pair of sandals that
showed off her fresh pedicure. Her stretched white
t-shirt exposed the fact that her nickel sized nipples
were erect.

"What up fellas?" She greeted as she made
her way to the porch.

"What's up girl?" Black responded with a
smile of approval before asking, "Where you going
looking like that?"

"Looking like what?" She challenged with a
wide grin.

"Girl, you know how you look?" Georgia

Slim replied with a smile of his own.

"Dam, ya'll make a bitch feel as if she be looking nasty all the time."

"It ain't like that," Georgia Slim assured, "we just use to you having some Air-Max and some Dickies on with a t-shirt or thermal. Now you walk down here with your hair, nails and feet done. You got one of those tight t-shirts on to show how horny you is, and you don't want us to say nothing? Now tell me what's really going?"

"It ain't nothing really," she blushed, "I guess you can say I'm trying to live a little better."

"Well, you definitely done did that," Black declared.

"So you like?" She asked with a little pizzazz.

"Yeah, you tight," Georgia Slim stressed, "but you already knew that."

"I came down here to see if Kruger here," she finally revealed.

"Now I see what's going," Georgia Slim replied while looking over at Black with a sinister grin.

"What is it you suppose to be seeing?" She inquired as if she really didn't know.

"Nothing," he replied with the same look, "but he ain't made it down yet, but I'll call and see where he at."

"I already tried to call him, but he ain't answering."

"His phone must be charging or something, cause you know if he don't do nothing else, he gonna answer that phone," Black implied.

"I need to holler at him cause I gotta get straight," she stressed with a disgruntled expression.

Georgia Slim and Black just looked at each other and burst out laughing.

"What the hell is ya'll laughing at?" Is what she demanded to know.

"Get straight in what way?" Black questioned as he tried to control his laughter.

"I need to holler at bra about this here, cause he know he needs to slow down," Georgia Slim stressed between chuckles.

"Dam ya'll, just make sure ya'll tell him that I need to see him," she stressed before sashaying back up towards Gunslanga's trap house.

"You know that nigga Kruger done broke her off?" Black stated as they watched her strut up the sidewalk.

****

"Deamon, what's wrong?" Teresa was asking from the passenger seat.

They had just left the hospital. She had called him complaining about she was feeling sick.

"It ain't nothing wrong," he replied in a nonchalant manner, "I just have a lot on my plate these days."

"Deamon, I'm keeping my baby!" She retorted with authority.

He looked over at her as if she had lost her mind before replying with, "Now who said you couldn't keep the child?"

"Our child, not the child!" She stressed.

"Girl you know what I'm trying to say!" He snapped back, "Could you try not to be so defensive about everything?"

"I'm sorry, I just thought," she started to say before he cut her off.

"Listen baby-girl," he lightly stated, clearly trying to keep his composure, "if we gonna be together, I never want to hear you say you're sorry again, just say you apologize."

"I'm sor," she started to say, "I mean, I apologize, but what's the difference?"

"Just listen to it, I'm sorry," he stated before pausing for a moment and adding, "If you was sorry, your ass wouldn't be in this truck with me."

This caused her to smile before she inquired, "You love me don't you?"

"Now where that come from?"

"Why you just can't answer the question, and how come you never tell me?"

A light smirk appeared on his face before he asked, "Have you ever heard me say that to anyone?"

"No actually I haven't, and I really think that's sad," she replied with a questionable expression.

"Well, I think it's sad that you can tell someone you love them and still treat them like shit. I feel that I don't have to tell that to nobody, I try to let my actions do my talking. Now would you rather for me to tell you or show you?"

"Why can't I get both?" She replied.

"Typical woman," he spat out with a sly grin before adding, "ya'll aint never satisfied."

"I can be satisfied," she interjected.

"So you're saying you're not now?"

"Now how did we switch from you telling me that you love me to whether or not I'm satisfied?"

"We'll talk about this later," he stressed before adding, "right now I have to get you back at the crib, cause I still have a few loose ends to tie up."

After hearing that, she didn't speak another word until they were in the apartment and he was about to walk out the door.

"I guess I'll see you tomorrow sometime, huh?"

He just looked back at her for a moment before shaking his head and walking out the door.

When he was in his truck he programmed the disc player until the sounds of Scarface blasted through the speakers.

The way he looked at it, things were already out of sync in his life and now Teresa was pregnant. It wasn't like he didn't want a baby from her, it was just that he knew he was with Teresa forever now.

STUCK

One wouldn't think that it was such a bad thing, but he knew that Teresa wasn't everything she claimed to be.

A lot of things puzzled him about her, like the fact that he knew, that she knew, that she was pregnant before she left the house for work. If she only knew that he had saw all three pregnancy sticks in the trash when he walked in the bathroom that morning, he wonder what she would've said in her defense.

It bothered him more than anything that she would attempt to play games with him, especially about her being pregnant. It made him really wonder what her deceiving limit was, or rather or not she had a limit. But despite all the drama she was bringing to the table, he still had business in the streets to look after, so his Teresa sagas would just have to unfold on their own.

After turning on his phone, he noticed that he had five messages. Three were from Kay-Kay, one was from Gunslanga and the other was from Georgia Slim. He called Gunslanga first.

"Yeah," Gunslanga answered.

"What's going playboy?" Kruger asked.

"Man, where you been?"

"Tending to this crazy ass broad."

"Who, Teresa?"

"Who else?"

"Listen playboy," Gunslanga stressed avoiding Kruger's last response, "I got everything right here, but I ain't gonna bring it myself. I want to send one of the twins with Amanda if it's alright with you."

"Whatever you wanna do." Kruger responded.

"Dam playboy, I know something is up now, cause I just knew that you were going to protest that move," Gunslanga revealed.

"But you still asked me?"

"You know it."

"That's why you didn't get any lip," Kruger brought to his attention, "if you already thought about what I'll say, you had to have some good reasons to still bring it to the table. Playboy, both of our cheese is involved, so if we lose, we lose together, and you already know that we ain't in a position to be losing nothing."

"My nigga you know I love ya right?" Gunslanga stressed.

"Whatever nigga," Kruger replied before asking, "where you at anyway?"

"The *La'Quinta.*"

"Look in the Lincoln under the passenger's floor mat, and you'll see a key. That's the key to Teresa's apartment down there. Go and stay there. I'm a send you some cheese for this month's rent and next month's bills, cause you know you don't need to be staying at no hotel."

"Yeah, hell yeah!" He excitedly responded, "I had done forgot all about that crib."

"I was keeping it for Teresa for when she moved back to Savannah, but her ass done turned up pregnant."

"And another one bites the dust," he replied with a light giggle.

"Yeah, that's what it sounds like to me too."

"I guess she got what she's been begging for."

"That's what it looks like," he replied before implying, "Kay-Kay must be dry or something because she done hit me up like three times?"

"Yeah, she called me asking where you were, so you might need to hit her up."

"True, but if you need something, hit me up."

"Keep the phone on."

"The only reason it was off then is I was with crazy ass Teresa at the hospital."

"True, just be safe out there playboy."

"You know that, much love playboy."

"Til death!" Gunslanga replied before the line went dead.

****

"Say Kruger," Black was saying, "you should've seen how Kay-Kay looked when she came through here looking for you the other day."

They sat in the middle room with Georgia Slim, Red and Rip, smoking on a blunt, while Vader was at the door and Butler was cutting the grass.

"Yeah playboy," Georgia Slim agreed, "she was looking right. Walking down here talking about she looking for you so that she can get straight," he added with a light chuckle.

"Dam nigga," Red stressed, "you knocking off Kay-Kay too?"

Kruger grinned before replying with, "Man, it ain't even like that."

"Man, you know that you done tapped that ass," Rip urged.

"Well, what's understood," is all he was able to get out before Red cut him off.

"Dam that there bra, how that pussy?"

"Man, I ain't about to go into all that," Kruger replied with a wide grin, "you tripping."

"I mean if she got that synthetic, let it be known," Red stated right before Vader called Kruger to the door.

When he reached the door, Vader pointed to the sidewalk where Kay-Kay was standing waiting on him.

"What's popping Kay-Kay?" He questioned as he walked towards her.

"I need to show you something," she responded with a seductive grin.

"Oh yeah, what up?"

"It's at the house," she replied as she started walking back towards Gunslanga's trap-house.

Kruger looked back at Vader and said, "Tell

the fellas that I'll be back, I'm just going down the street."

As soon as they reached the corner of Summer and Hopkins Street, the narcotic squad pulled in front of them.

"Mr. Pearsey, do you think that we can get you and your lady friend to put ya'll hands on the hood of this car?" Honeycutt asked after stepping out of the lead car.

Besides the blue Lumina that Honeycutt had jumped out of, there were two Blazers, a black and blue one.

"Na'll, but I don't mind putting my hands on the trunk," Kruger attested, "cause it ain't no way in hell on putting my hands on that hot ass hood."

"I wish you would try and run!" One of the agents said to him.

"Run, for what?!" Kruger retorted, "You ain't gonna run from me, so what I look like running from you?"

"Since you have so much to say why don't you tell us where your friend Gunslanga is," the agent stated in a sarcastic manner.

"Didn't they just find some people dead for what you asking me to do?" He responded with a sly grin.

The agent then dug in his pockets and pulled out his cell phone, his license and a roll of money.

"How much is that?" Honeycutt asked him.

"It's a little over 350," Kruger replied, "it just looks big. You know I gotta get my flex on, how else you think I can get females like this?"

"Why do you have all these small bills?" The agent asked.

"Why do you ask so many questions?" Kruger retorted.

"They're clean so let them go," Honeycutt ordered his crew before turning his attention back to Kruger, "Just remember you little shit, you're gonna fuck around and fuck up, just like your homie."

Kruger just shook his head as he watched Honeycutt and his goons get back in their cars.

Right before Honeycutt got in his car he turned to Kruger and said, "By the way let him know that I asked about him."

"Consider it done. Just don't harass the wrong person today," he replied before he and Kay-Kay headed turning back towards Gunslanga's trap-house.

As they walked up the steps of the house Kruger's phone rang.

"You alright bra?" Black asked in a concerned tone.

"Yeah, I'm good playboy. They drove right by the house, so ya'll should be good too."

"Alright bra, be safe out there."

"You already know."

"Much love."

"Til death, big homie," Kruger stressed before hanging up.

"My bad," Kay-Kay apologized as she walked in the kitchen, "I guess I picked a bad time, huh?"

"You're alright, but what up?" He responded as he followed her in the kitchen.

"My scale is fucking up and I wanted you to check it out for me," she replied as she grabbed from out of the drawer and placed it on the small kitchen table.

"It probably just needs some batteries," he stated as he toyed with it.

A few moments later he said, "Yeah, it's the

batteries."

"So how am I suppose to get my grind on without a scale?"

"I got you, just chill for a minute," he replied as headed for the door.

She met him at the door and said, "I was hoping you had me all the way around."

"Now that depends on how you act," he responded before pulling away from her and walking out the door.

-TERESA-

Now I knew that his ass wasn't coming home last night! When I called, he didn't even have the decency to answer the phone! I just can't let him continue to treat me like shit!

He is suppose to take me to Charlotte next month, but I bet we don't go. Something is gonna come up. Something always comes up! Lord knows that I'm tired of things always coming up when it's time to be with me.

I talked to Toya about it. I was looking for her to say talk to him or something in that range, but she flat out said leave the nigga alone. Now what really gives her the right to tell me that? Now what type of shit is that to tell me!

She went on and on about how I let the young nigga play me and how I didn't even let David do that to me. She's always bringing up David's ass. It's like she's forgotten how she and ole sucka ass Eddie plotted together to get him locked up. If you ask me, I'm the fool for calling her ass for her opinion.

I can tell that at times she's real jealous of the fact that Deamon gives me what I want and Ron don't have it like that. But what she fails to realize is that I'm the one who's jealous. I mean Ron might not have that much money, but at least he's home every night.

"Officer Davis, your needed in medical," is what I hear over the intercom.

You know it's really crazy how we really don't respect the relationships we're in, until we're no longer in them. I admit, David was sort of good to me, so I would be lying if I said I didn't miss some of the things he did for me. But the reality is, I'm with Deamon now. So sue me for wanting our relationship to better than me and David's was. I mean you're suppose to make it better than the last time. But I get the feeling that Deamon isn't feeling that too funny.

"What up Officer Davis?" I hear one of the inmates yell as I pass his building, "I know that nigga treating your fine ass right!"

****

Jimmy, Weasel, Ericka and Surina sat inside of The Olive Garden with empty pasta dishes in front of them. Jimmy was on his third shot of Hennessey while Weasel was on his second. The girls were drinking on Bacardi Razz, so they all were a little tipsy.

"We might as well go and get a room," Weasel was saying to Ericka.

"You already know that I'm down," Ericka acknowledged.

"I guess we all can hit the same hotel," Surina stressed as she gazed over at Jimmy, "cause I definitely have to have me some tonight."

"I second that there," Ericka agreed with a glooming expression.

"Jim-bo, you might need some help with

316

her tonight," Weasel stressed as he gallantly eyed her, "she looks as if she's ready for the world."

Jimmy just stuck his chest out and announced, "I never met a woman I couldn't handle."

Weasel just lightly chuckled before saying, "Well, I'm here to let you know that they're out there, I mean they're definitely out there."

They all raised from their seats and made their way towards the exit. As they walked through the first door, Kruger and Deidra were walking through the last.

"Hey Deamon," Surina seductively greeted.

"What up," he replied.

"You!" She stressed with authority.

Everyone froze for a moment before Weasel finally broke the ice, "What's going kinfolk?"

"Shit, just maintaining," Kruger replied in a cool manner as he embraced Weasel.

"What up Jimmy?" Kruger asked after seeing how uncomfortable he was, "You think that ya'll ready to see me and my folks on that court again?"

STUCK

Jimmy heard Kruger, but his mind was too focused on Surina, but he still replied with, "Oh yeah, anytime ya'll ready, we can get down."

Deidra then spoke to Weasel and Jimmy before she walked through the last door to find the waiter only to see Surina following her.

"Dam Deidra," Surina stressed as she caught up with her, "me and you were suppose to be better than this, I mean we've been friends for too long. I don't have no animosity about nothing, even though you pulled a Jerry Springer move on me."

Deidra just gave her a devilish grin before she replied with "You know, I wouldn't care if we was born friends."

She wanted to add the fact that she was pregnant with his baby so there was really no hope for them to ever be friends again. But out of respect of Kruger's wishes, she held her tongue.

Surina walked up to her and stressed, "Bitch, you're a thug hoe, I made what he sees! I made you, and this is how you repay me?! Oh bitch, I'll get him back!"

Before Deidra could utter a word, she had already walked away.

As she walked past Kruger she stressed, "Hope to see you soon."

At that time her and Kruger were the only two in that small space so he replied with, "You need to stop tripping before ole boy tear your head off."

"I want you to remember one thing," she stressed as she walked up to him, "I belong to you, not him."

Kruger just shook his head and walked away. He could smell the liquor on her breath, so he figured that it had to be the liquor that had her tripping like she was.

(CHAPTER 11)

"*I didn't* appreciate how you just walked out of here last month," Mr. Singleton was saying to Kruger from behind his desk in the parole office.

"I don't mean any disrespect, but I have a long day ahead of me," Kruger replied with a look of frustration, "now, if you have a problem with the money, you need to address that."

"Just calm down," he nervously replied, "all I'm saying is that we need to be a little more discreet with this. As soon as you walked out of my office last month, another officer came in and saw the five hundred dollars on my desk. Now she didn't say anything, but I've caught her watching me a few times since then."

"You have my number," Kruger replied, "just give me a call me when you get off and I'll have someone meet you with it."

"That's all I was asking," he claimed with a phony smile, "just try to keep your nose clean as possible, because I can't overlook everything."

"You just make sure you play your position and I'll play mine," Kruger replied before putting the 25 dollar money order on his desk.

"I'll call you tonight."

"Have a nice day Mr. Singleton," he stated before stepping out of the office.

Deidra was in the parking-lot waiting for him. It was 9:30 in the morning and neither of the two had eaten yet, so when he stepped in the car that was the first thing she spoke about.

"Baby, let's go to I-Hop before you check in on the Summer," she suggested.

"I'm cool with that," he agreed as he dug in his pocket and pulled out the five hundred for Singleton, "do you have any money on you?"

"Yeah, a little."

"Well, you might have to pay for breakfast, because I need you to hold this money, so that you can give it to my parole officer when he calls later."

"Just put it in my purse," she replied as she pulled out of the parking-lot.

STUCK

Red walked out of the middle room of 1122 with a blunt right before the sounds of 2- Pac's, 'Thug Life', hummed through the walls.

"Man, ya'll already know what time it is!" He stressed after walking on the porch.

"Yeah playboy, it's all about that cheese today," Hamburger replied with a sly grin as he cuddled a 5th of *Hennessy* in his usual spot.

Among them were Black, Rip, Georgia Slim and Big Ox.

"Man, I just got off the phone with Kruger, so it's on and popping!" Red added with a golden smile.

"He must have told you something good," Black implied.

"He ain't told me nothing, I just know my nigga gonna look out," he stated before pausing and adding, "besides fool, this here is my month."

"Like I told you the other day," Georgia Slim stressed, "if it's yours, I'll be right there with you."

"That just means that I'll have a down ass nigga to climb with," Red stated before they gave each other dap.

"I'm right there too," Black interjected, "what fool on the Summer ain't trying to see better days?"

"Man, it's the first of the month and we getting fire ass prices right now," Hamburger mentioned, "so it's time out for playing. If you ain't got a brick by the end of the month, you're considered as a peasant."

"In order to stack it, you must claim it," Red added.

"Well, let's claim the middle room with that blunt before we be trying to get out of 401 again," Hamburger instructed.

"My bad," Red replied as they all walked down the hall, leaving Georgia Slim on the porch.

It was only 10:30 in the morning and he had already made 450. He smiled at that thought as he saw a guy coming from Gurley's parking-lot. Georgia Slim could tell that he was a smoker from how his pace speeded up after seeing him.

"What's going nephew?" The guy greeted after reaching the porch.

"What's going unk?" Georgia Slim replied.

"Do you think you could hook me up with

something nice for a hundred?"

"I gotcha unk," he replied as he rose from the stoop and lead him in the house, "just step in the first room on the left," he added as he closed and locked the front door and gate.

All of the fellas called the smokers unk or auntie. They couldn't possibly remember all of their clients names, so instead of saying crack head or junkie, they attempted to show respect.

Georgia Slim was on his way back from the kitchen when he heard a knock at the door.

"Who that?" He asked.

"A Summer Street warrior!" The familiar voice stressed from the other side.

"Just give me a second bra," he replied.

"I'm dirty, bra!"

Georgia Slim opened the door in record time and Kruger stepped in with a black duffle bag.

"Dam playboy, you moving in?" he joked.

"You can say that," Kruger replied with a light smile as he walked in the first room with his comrade right behind him.

"Here you go unk," Georgia Slim stated as he handed the smoker the product.

"Yeah, yeah, nephew, that's why I like dealing with you," the guy excitedly proclaimed as he gave him the money.

After escorting him out and locking the front door again, he rejoined Kruger in the first room.

"What was that, the ole 1.5 for a hundred lick?" Kruger asked with a sly grin.

"Na'll, the ole 1.3," Georgia Slim replied with a smile.

"Dam, you doing better than me."

"You know all they need to see is a nice piece and they're automatically overjoyed," he implied as he took a seat on the couch by the window.

"You about ready to ree-up?" Kruger questioned after pulling out a package and placing it on the table.

"Yeah, just let me catch another sale like that, cause all I got is forty-four hundred right now, so I'm a dollar short," he replied with as he reached in his pocket.

"I know you ain't sitting in here with forty-four hundred in your pocket?"

"Hell na'll, all my bread is across the street," he replied as he pulled out his loose change.

STUCK

"Just give me the forty-four, and throw me the dollar when you get it."

"Say no more," Georgia Slim stressed before he rose from the couch and walked out.

Kruger grabbed his phone and called Deidra.

"Yes baby," she answered.

"I need you to meet me in Gurley's parking-lot in ten minutes."

"I'm already out here, I stopped to get you some orange juice."

He couldn't help but smile before saying, "I'll be over there in ten minutes."

After hanging up, he walked down the hall to the middle room where 2-Pac was clearly chanting, *"I'm up before the sunrise, first to hit the block."*

"Dam playboy, when you got here?" Black asked with a surprised expression.

"Just now," he stated before asking, "who ya'll got watching the door?"

"Vader," Red replied, "he just ran to Bennet Lane to take a quick shower."

"That's what's up," he replied before asking, "but is everybody straight, cause I got ole

326

girl waiting outside."

"Na'll playboy, I definitely gotta holler at you," Red raised up and stressed.

"I might as well get a little something too," Black raised up and added.

"Let me holla at him first and we'll call you when we're through," Red insisted.

After they stepped in the first room, Kruger asked, "So what up bra?"

"You think that I can get a half for the nine?"

"I see you ain't trying to play no more."

"The way I see it, it's either now or never," Red responded with a wide grin as Kruger handed him the package.

"You should be able to bring back no less than twenty-five with that there," Kruger mentioned before Red ran up the hallway to get the money.

"Say Black, what up with you?" Kruger stressed after Red brought back the money.

At the same time Georgia Slim was walking back in the house with the forty-four hundred.

"So what it is, brother Black?" He asked

after they stepped in the room.

"I gotta fuck with another quarter, but when I get back at you, I'm grabbing a half."

Five minutes later Kruger was walking towards Gurley's where Deidra was patiently waiting.

"You miss me already?" She asked with a sly grin as he sat in the car.

"And you know it!" he responded as he dug in his cargo pockets and pulled out a brown paper bag before asking, "How much money you got on you?"

"A little over two hundred, plus the five you want me to give your P.O."

"You got something you trying to buy today?"

"No, not really."

"Well, I need like a hundred of it to put in this bag to make eighteen."

Without a word spoken she dug in her purse, reached for her wallet and pulled out a hundred dollar bill.

"Now I need for you to take this and put it up for me," he implied.

"Alright."

He then reached for the door handle to get out and she pulled him back and stressed, "Aren't you forgetting something?"

He smiled at her before he leaned over and passionately kissed her.

When they finally separated, she licked her lips with a smile of her own before saying, "That's not what I was talking about."

She then reached in the backseat and grabbed the orange juice.

After he kissed her on the cheek and was getting out she stressed, "Call me if you need anything."

He then walked around to the driver side and replied with, "You know I am, I mean who else I'm gonna call?"

At that moment Kruger felt that he could take on the world with a woman like Deidra. After walking back to 1122 and seeing that Vader had made it back, he called Kay-Kay.

****

The moment Kay-Kay hung up with Kruger she started cleaning up everything in sight, so by the time he walked through the door with Vader, she was washing the dishes.

Vader had a bag over his shoulder that Kruger grabbed from him before he said, "I need you to go to Butler's mama house and tell him he needs to grab the door at the house, cause me and you gonna work this house right here."

"You know that I don't work for crumbs!" Vader stressed as if he was negotiating a million dollar deal.

"And you of all people should know that I don't pay in crumbs."

Without another word spoken Vader was out the door.

Kruger locked the door behind him and secured it with the two by four braces Butler had made for Gunslanga.

After securing the door, he stepped in the kitchen with the bag and asked Kay-Kay, "Now what you working with?"

She turned around and started to undress. First she took off her tight t-shirt and allowed her breast to get some breathing room. She then kicked off her sandals and pulled down her shorts along with the pink pair of thongs she had on, revealing the fact that her pubic hairs were closely shaven.

"Now you know what I meant," Kruger managed to utter out.

She then placed her fingers on the outer creases of her pussy before she stressed, "Now do you see how wet you got me?"

He couldn't do anything but gaze at her as she walked over to him. With the confidence of a porn star, she unbuttoned his jeans and pulled them and his boxers down.

"Can you tell me why he never complains when I'm around?" She asked with a sly grin as she dropped to her knees.

"Now that's something you have to ask him," he replied in an attempt to hold his composure.

She made it her business to keep eye contact with him as she inserted him in her mouth. It was more of a sexual war the way their eyes stayed focused on each other.

Before you knew it, she was sitting on the edge of the kitchen table with her legs spread.

When he entered her, she dug her nails in his back. As he started to plunge her, she was whimpering and moaning out his name. After a few moments passed, he picked her up and started thrusting her on top of him.

Despite her lack of control she was determined not to let him get the best of her as she continued to slam down harder and harder on his dick. He knew that she was getting closer and closer to erupting because he wasn't too far from the same act.

"Dam Kruger!" Is what she managed to stutter out as her juices flowed all over his mid section.

It was like he paid the stiffness of her body no attention because he continued to plunge hard and deep into her.

"Aaahhhh!" He finally screamed out after pulling out of her and releasing his juices on the floor.

"You didn't have to pull out," she stated as he placed her on the table.

He looked at her as if she had lost her mind before finally replying with, "You ain't ready for that, because I ain't ready for that."

She just shook her head lightly before a sly smirk appeared on her face. She then jumped off the table, grabbed her clothes and headed for the bathroom with him right behind her. In the bathroom she cleaned them both off. The moment she finished him, he went in the kitchen and cleaned his juices off the floor.

"I would've got that up," she stated after walking in the kitchen.

"I got it," he replied before slapping her on her naked ass.

"You must have known that I'm a pain freak," she stressed as she bent over and exposed the fact that she was still wet.

He just shook his head before he said, "If you don't put your clothes on, we ain't gonna be able to make a dime in here."

"You right," she replied with a seductive smile as she headed towards the bathroom.

When she came back a few minutes later, she knew that he was right back in grind mode because the first thing he asked was, "Where the beakers?"

She reached under the sink and grabbed the two chemical beakers.

"So, how much you working with?" He asked after she handed him the beakers.

"I got like fifty-five hundred, but I owe Slanga a stack."

"I'll tell you what," he started to say as he grabbed a package out of his bag, "I'm gonna let you get 190 grams for the forty-five, and you can give me Slanga's stack, and I'll make sure he get it."

"Are you gonna help me cook it up?" She pleaded.

"What you think I'm here for?"

"You know that you don't want me to answer that," she replied with a sly grin.

"Where Prime at?" He asked, "Slanga say he owes him four stacks."

"He should have it, but if he comes through it'll probably be later on," she replied.

"Well, me and you will rotate until he gets back," Kruger stressed with a serious expression before adding, "it's time out for playing, it's time to get this money."

-KRUGER-

Here it is Wednesday morning, so a warrior has been at it for two days. I started out with seven bricks, now I'm halfway through. I'm still down here at Slanga's trap trying to turn seven bricks to twenty in a week.

That cat Prime came through the other night and drop three stacks off, so he still owe Slanga one. He say he grinding over at a spot the streets call, The Cut, so me and Kay-Kay been holding the trap down while Vader been securing the porch.

I let Vader sit out there with a quarter ounce so he catching all the dime and nick sales. He already know that me and Kay-Kay get any sale that's 15 or better, even though I know he has short stopped a few dub sales. But who am I to complain, he reeing- up with me.

Me and Kay-Kay's freaky ass done bumped heads again, but I had to let her know that we gotta lust for this bread right now. She seems to understand, but you never know what her freaky ass will do next.

She was happy with the ten ounces I

335

cooked up for her. She almost working with eight stacks, and I think she still got an ounce left. And they wonder why it's hard for a soldier to stay away from Summer Street.

Red, Hamburger and the rest of the fellas down the street trying to make a dollar out of fifteen cent. It's like every real weight sale that come through, they sending them down here to me. But like I said before, who am I to complain. The crazy thing is, I haven't seen them folks riding.

I talked to Slanga and Firebug and they say that we should hold off on that information for when we really need it. I can feel where they coming from, but I've been itching to hit one of these oppressors up. I done even took the liberty of riding past Honeycutt house.

I saw his wife, Patricia, walk out and get the mail. Ole girl look like she Latino or something. She holding too! It's hard for me to see how he coped her. She must had to marry him to stay in the country or some shit like that. But, I'm gonna let that go for now, cause just like Firebug said, our money ain't right for all of that.

Now with everything that's going on, my mama just called me and told me that my sister pregnant. The funny thing about it is, I didn't even know that she was fucking. I guess the old saying is true, what you do in the dark, always comes to the light.

My mama probably ain't doing nothing but snapping on her about it. That's my mama for you. Sooner or later she'll realize that all the yelling she doing ain't gonna stop her from being pregnant.

Tamika has to know that she good though. I mean a playa gonna do whatever for her baby. She's just in that stage where she realizes she's disappointed a few people. But hell, life is full of disappointments.

★★★★★★★★★★★★★★

Hamburger, Red and Black where all on the porch accommodating the Friday afternoon fiend traffic when a black Benz pulled right in front of 1122. The driver stepped out of the car and all three of them recognized him immediately.

"Big Jay!" Hamburger excitedly greeted.

"What up fellas?" The huge guy replied as he stepped towards the porch.

Big Jay was at least 6'4 and weighed around 330lbs.He played on defensive behind Gilbert

Brown for the Green Bay Packers. He was one of the few pro players from Augusta, along with Will Avery and Deon Grant, who always made it their business to holler at the fellas on the street whenever they were in town. But out of all them, the fellas saw more of Big Jay because he just happened to be Gunslanga's older brother.

"What's going Hamburger?" Big Jay stressed as he embraced him.

"I need to be asking you that, you the one pulling up in a Benz," Burger replied with a genuine smile.

"Man, that ain't mine, that's Slanga shit. I just snatched it from my mama's house."

"You bullshitting!" Hamburger retorted.

"I wish I was," Big Jay replied, "because that bitch rides real tight," he stated as Red and Black jumped off the porch to embrace the big man.

"How long you here for this time, big homie?" Black asked.

"I was just stopping through, until my mama told me that them folks looking for my brother again. So you know I gotta see what's up with that before I dip," he replied in a concerned manner.

"Say Red," Hamburger stressed, "call Kruger and tell him that Big Jay down here."

"You mean to tell me that they let that fool out?" Big Jay replied with a wide grin.

"Yeah," Red stressed, "he right down the street at Slanga crib."

"Don't call him, just get in and we gonna ride down there," Big Jay stressed before he got back in the Benz with Red on the passenger side.

When they pulled up to Gunslanga's trap house, Vader was sitting on the porch.

"Say Vader," Red stressed, "tell Kruger to come here right fast."

"Say Kruger," Vader called through the window.

"Yeah," they heard him reply.

"Red and some big ass ugly nigga out here for you," Vader replied with a gruesome expression.

When Kruger stepped through the door and saw Big Jay sitting on the Benz he yelled out, "What up big homie?"

"What's up ole black ass fool?" Big Jay replied as Kruger reach out and bumped fist with him.

"I would give you a hug big bra, but my personal hygiene ain't up to par right now," Kruger responded.

"Look at this fool done grew up and coped him a vocabulary," Big Jay replied with a smile of approval.

"They say make it better than the last time," Kruger responded with a smile.

"I can feel that," Big Jay replied before asking, "so when the last time you heard from Hammah?"

"I talk to him every now and then at Bad-Azz's baby-mama's house."

"When ya'll two fools together a nigga best to walk a straight line," he stressed with a light chuckle.

"You know it," Kruger assured before adding, "but you know it ain't no difference solo, he holding his and I'm definitely holding mine."

"Now that's what's up," Red stressed.

"So where Slanga at?" Big Jay asked.

"Now that's something I have to holler at you about later," Kruger replied before changing the subject, "but I see that you done coped a Benz?"

"This Slanga shit," he responded, "he ain't tell you he coped this either?"

"He told me that he had something to bust heads with, but I never thought that he'd do it like that."

"I just stole it out of my mama's driveway," Big Jay stressed.

"He ain't too funny gonna like that," Red implied.

"That nigga can't whup my ass!" Big Jay stressed.

"My sister should be through in a minute to scoop me up, so I guess I'll shower up and we'll do something tonight," Kruger implied.

"That's straight, because I have to hollar at you about Slanga anyway," Big Jay replied as he jumped back in the Benz.

"Get my number from Red and hit me around six, dinner on me," Kruger stressed as Red got in the passenger seat.

"You just make sure you be ready, cause you already know I like to eat," Big Jay replied.

341

"Just hit me," Kruger stressed before Big Jay pulled off.

"So that's Slanga's brother, huh?" Vader asked with a smirk, "I guess all them niggas big and ugly," he added causing Kay-Kay, who was obviously eased dropping, to burst out laughing.

"Somebody gonna hurt you about that mouth," Kruger implied with a light chuckle of his own.

"I wish a muthafucka would!" Vader stressed before Kruger cut him off.

"You wish a muthafucka would what, muthafucka!" He questioned as he stepped towards Vader.

"See, I can't even kick it with you," Vader stressed as he balled up, "I told you to stop being so serious about everything," he added as Kruger shook his head and headed back in the house, "you're dumb ass is gonna fuck around and have a stroke at the tender age of 21, dummy!"

"You know to dam much!" Kruger stated as he closed and locked the door behind him.

"And your dumb ass don't know enough!" Vader replied before adding, "And nigga don't talk me to death through this window either, be a man and say what you have to say to me in my face!"

"If I was to come out there all your ass gonna do is run," Kruger stressed.

"That might be so, but since you ain't came yet, I can still talk shit!"

"Shut the fuck up Vader," Kay-Kay insisted, "I'm trying to watch my stories."

"Girl, if I didn't like that little ass that keeps following you around, I'd snap on your fine ass too. But since I do wanna hit that, I'll chill for a minute," he replied causing Kruger to burst out laughing.

****

"Say fool," Big Jay was saying to his brother on the phone as him and Kruger rode in Kruger's truck, headed towards T.G.I. Friday's, "are you good down there?"

"Yeah bra," Gunslanga replied, "I'm just trying to stay out of sight for a few."

"Why is it every time I come home you in the mist of some bullshit?" Big Jay stressed.

"Things aren't always as bad as they seem," Gunslanga replied, "it just looks that way when you're on the outside looking in."

"I'll go for that for now, but if you need anything, just get at me."

"I might need you to check on this cat for me," Gunslanga implied.

"And do what?" Big Jay questioned.

"See if money really do make the world go round."

"True dat," he replied with a wide grin, "I just gotta find out where he at."

"Kruger already got that, I just need you to handle the negotiating."

"Consider it done," he replied, "but if you need anything else, make sure you get at me."

"I'm good for now, but I'll get at you if something comes up."

"Yeah, you got the number."

"Vice-versa," Gunslanga replied before the line went dead.

Big Jay looked over at Kruger and asked, "Now when are ya'll muthafuckas gonna get it together?"

"You know big homie," Kruger replied with a serious expression, "every nigga ain't blessed with a wicked jump shot or got the ability to chase down the quarterback on every down."

"You think that you're telling me something I don't know?" Big Jay questioned, "I had to struggle to get where I'm at, and when it all boils down I'm still second string, so you think I'm comfortable with that? But I'm still going at it hard, until I feel comfortable. I just pray that a nigga still possess enough will power to continue to go hard at it even when I start feeling comfortable."

"I feel you big homie, because it's a lot of shit I wanna do with my life too," Kruger revealed, "and don't get it twisted, I ain't blind to the fact that I could never be comfortable living like this. But the thing is I'm living right now. It might not be a well-respected life to most, but it's my life, my nigga. I just don't wanna end up out here like these other cats I see, just existing out here. This is what paying the bills, big homie. When my mama needs something, she knows that it ain't nothing for her to call me to get it, ya heard."

Big Jay just looked over at his young friend and shook his head before stressing, "Sometimes you gotta be selfish as hell, cause it's too many leeches out here. Everybody wanna be your friend for all the wrong reasons. It's all about who you are and the status they achieve by knowing you."

345

"Point seen big homie," Kruger stated as he pulled in to the restaurant's parking-lot.

"I wish that I could take all ya'll to Green Bay with me."

"Man, ain't nobody moving up there in the freezing cold!" Kruger retorted as they both stepped out of the truck.

Big Jay chuckled and replied with, "Why do you think they make heaters and jackets?"

"We need to get up there to hollar at some of them broads," Kruger stressed with a smile.

"It ain't nothing up there but snow bunnies," Big Jay replied as they walked in the restaurant.

"You know that they ain't my thing, I love the sisters," Kruger replied as he led the way to the bar.

"When you see how thick they is, you gonna swear they sisters," Big Jay replied with a sly grin of his own.

****

"How much you working with?" Weasel was asking Pimp over the phone.

346

"The usual," Pimp replied.

"Dam cuz-o," Weasel stressed, "you gotta start bringing more to the table."

"Fuck you mean, bring more to the table?" Pimp retorted.

"Dam playa," he replied with a little irritation, "where do all your cheddar go?"

"You checking my pockets now?" Pimp questioned.

"It ain't even like that," Weasel replied, "I'm just saying, I've been feeding you lovely prices for over a month. Now here it is the first of the month and you still coping the same shit! Now you hurting my pockets."

"You know my nigga, I really ain't gotta fuck with you, I can fuck with Kruger or Slanga!"

"See there you go with the bullshit. A nigga been stop playing games with this here. Real hustlers let their money do the talking. If you stop tricking so much, you could probably be in that category."

"Dam, it sound as if you hating on a playa?" Pimp sarcastically implied.

"All I'm saying is, if you want that big eighth come up with four more dollars."

"I guess Pac was right after all," Pimp stated with aggression, "they really do fake like they your homies, but they phony muthafuckas!"

"Be easy," Weasel replied in a humble manner.

"If you ask me, it's too many wanna be Nino Brown's out here!"

"If you was smart, you'll be trying to become one too. It's better than playing Pookey, and you ain't but twenty-six hundred from being on that level!" Weasel stressed before hanging the phone up.

Within seconds he was dialing Kruger's number.

"Speak, or forever hold yours," Kruger answered.

"What up, this Weasel."

"What up with you?"

"I just got off the phone with that nigga Pimp."

"And?"

"This nigga tells me that I'm phony and then he goes on to say that he's tired of all these wanna-be Nino Brown's out here."

"So what are you looking for me to do about it?"

"Check this homie," Weasel stated before taking a deep breath, "that's my blood, and if I don't wanna continue to pacify him with this shit, that's on me. The only reason I'm hitting you with this is to let you know what's going. Pimp so shady that he might tell ya'll anything and have the whole Summer sour at a nigga."

"I feel you," Kruger replied, "I'll make sure I let the fellas know what the business is."

"Preciate that playboy."

"Ain't nothing."

"Where you at anyway? I just saw your truck go up Meadowbrook."

"I'm down the way, that's Big Jay in my truck."

"Oh yeah, tell that huge gorilla I said what up."

"Done deal, and don't lose no sleep on that, you good."

"Say no more, big homie," Weasel replied before stressing, "but make sure you be safe down there."

STUCK

"Alright homie," Kruger replied before hanging up.

Kruger was sitting on the couch vibing to the sounds of Goodie Mob's, 'Soul Food', while Vader held his position on the porch.

He couldn't see why Pimp was so caught up in burning all of his bridges, but what had his mind really boggling was how Weasel always called him about situations that really never concerned him. But in a way he understood where he was coming from.

He knew that Pimp was a time bomb sprinting through the game of life. The only question that crossed his mind was, who was gonna blow up with him when his time ran out? Pimp was a good dude, in his own way. The thing about it was, in the game you can't have it your own way. There are codes to acknowledge. He just hoped that Pimp would find a way to acknowledged them before they acknowledged him.

Kruger's concentration went from Pimp to the hundred-fifty thousand that he had hustled up that week. He was proud of himself for accomplishing his goal of grinding for the week, because in his eyes, it paid off. The best thing about it was, he still had a kilo put up, and that didn't include the half of kilo he was working out of at the moment. Now his only mission was to go through that half of kilo and make his way to Savannah.

(CHAPTER 12)

It was Stacy and Tracy's birthday and Firebug was walking out of Oglethorpe Mall with two custom bracelets that he just picked up from his jeweler. He'd noticed the two younger cats watching his every move while he was in the mall, but he really never paid them that much attention, at least not until he saw them following him to the parking lot.

The moment Firebug reached his Seville, he attempted to call Big Wade, but he never answered. As he pulled out he looked at the grey Maxima they were in and noticed the Fulton county tag, so that's when he called Gunslanga.

"Where you at, youngblood?" He questioned after Gunslanga answered.

"I'm over at Godfather's Pizza over here in this plaza on Victory drive."

"I know where you at," Firebug confirmed, "I'm on my way over there. Do you have some heat with you?"

"You already know it," Gunslanga responded, "but what up?"

"I got two fools tailing me and they been following me since I was in the mall," he finally revealed.

"What kind of car they in?"

"It's a grey Maxima with Fulton county tags."

"Don't worry Pop, just roll through and we'll find out who these fools is," Gunslanga stressed.

"I'll be there in the next ten minutes."

"When you get here just step out the car and walk in the pizza joint," Gunslanga directed.

"Alright, I'll be there in a few minutes," he stated before he hung up.

When Firebug finally pulled in the plaza, he parked right next to Amanda's Altima, while the goons parked a few spaces from him. Firebug hopped out of the car as if he never noticed them. When he reached the door Gunslanga walked out and they passed each other as if they were strangers.

353

STUCK

Gunslanga walked straight to their car and pulled out one of Kruger's twins and put it to the driver's head before stressing, "Now, I ain't gonna say this but one time. What I need ya'll to do is throw your fire in the back seat."

The passenger quickly obeyed by grabbing his Baby Uzi from under the seat and doing what he was told.

"Now with your friend moving at dam near the speed of lightning, I just know you understood what I said, because you're right here in front of me," he calmly implied to the driver.

The driver then eased his hand under the seat and grabbed a Desert Eagle, from the butt of the handle, and tossed it in the backseat.

"Now, if I was to pull ya'll out and search ya'll, it's best that I don't find no more pistols, cause that would only bring automatic church singing and flower bringing," he assured with a cold stare.

"That's all there is!" The driver professed.

"Does he speak for both of ya'll?" Gunslanga asked the passenger.

He just nodded his head, and that's when Gunslanga knew that he was the weaker of the

354

two.

"What I need you to do now is open this back door," he calmly ordered.

When he was in the back seat he called Amanda and stressed, "You know what to do."

The moment Gunslanga saw her and Firebug step out of the pizza joint he said, "Now, what I need for ya'll to do is follow the same car ya'll been following."

As Amanda and Firebug got in their cars the driver stuttered out, "Man, we ain't been following nobody!"

"Whatever playboy, just follow the rusty looking colored Caddy then!" He replied in a nonchalant manner.

As they rode in silence Gunslanga noticed that the driver was quickly perspiring and the passenger was trembling in his seat so he stressed, "Ya'll need to calm down, because if ya'll have the right answers to some very important question, ya'll probably make it out of this alive."

Moments later Amanda was leading the way in The La'Quinta's parking-lot off of Abercorn. After parking, she hopped out and went inside while Firebug made his way over to the Maxima.

"Alright, let's hear it," is what he practically commanded as he settled in the backseat.

"Say playboy!" Gunslanga stressed as he slapped the passenger across the head, "This is your time to speak!"

"Man, we ain't even from here!" He declared.

"And!" Firebug retorted, "Ya'll know what I wanna know, so don't try to play me for slow. From now on, it's best you answer my questions immediately!"

At that time Amanda was walking towards the Maxima. When she reached the car she handed Gunslanga a room key and stressed, "Ya'll in room 142, it's on the far left of the hotel, call me if you need me."

"You heard her," Firebug stressed, "drive until you find the room!"

After pulling in front of the room, Gunslanga handed Firebug the key and told him to get out with the passenger and open the door. Moments later all four men was secured in the small room.

"Now who sent ya'll?" Firebug

questioned with a sly grin.

Both of the men looked at each other and said nothing, so Gunslanga slapped the driver hard across the face with the Desert Eagle.

"Wrong answer," Firebug humbly stated with that same sly grin.

"Why should we tell you anything, when you still gonna kill us?" The driver declared.

That was the last word he ever spoke. Gunslanga put the nose of the huge pistol to his temple and pulled the trigger, causing his brain to be splattered on the headboard and walls.

The room was silent for a moment, as even Firebug, had to regain his composure after what he had just witnessed. It took a moment for him to swallow the lump in his throat and continue his investigation.

"Now your friend here had all the wrong answers, I just hope that you're able to conjure up some right ones."

Firebug noticed how the guy just stare at his friends remains as he looked over at Gunslanga with a shocked expression before he asked him, "Now who sent you?!"

They guy looked over at Firebug and

mumbled something that neither Gunslanga nor Firebug could understand, so Gunslanga put the nose of the pistol to his temple and pointed out, "I'm getting very irritated with this here."

"I said Wade," he finally stuttered out.

Firebug looked over at his protégé before standing up and walking towards the guy and saying, "Look here man, what's your name?"

"Michael."

"Well listen Michael, I'm having a little trouble with the name you gave me."

"I said Wade!" He retorted, "The man name is Wade!" He confirmed knowing that he'd violated the number one code of his profession.

In his heart, Michael had nothing else to live for, so the codes he once lived by was irrelevant at the moment. He'd dedicated his life to doing hits, but now he was feeling what some of his targets must have felt right before he pulled the trigger on them.

"Where is this Wade from?" Firebug interrogated.

"He has to be from here, I mean, this is where he called us from."

"So, how did he pay you?"

"He gave us ten grand up front and when we eliminated you, we were suppose to receive 15 more."

"So where are you suppose to meet him?"

"At the bus station."

"Any specific time?"

"No, just when we got rid of you," he replied with no emotion.

"Dam!" He spat out as he sat back down and took a deep breath before adding, "Listen Michael, I'm about to offer you a way out of this. I just need you to call up this Wade, just as if you have finished the job."

Michael just nodded his head before Firebug went on to say, "See, you've lucked up and came across an old school playa. So if everything is what you say it is, I'll let you live and clear the 15 grand that you were promised. Now, I know that you probably gonna miss your friend here, but it's a little too late to be tripping on him."

"So all you want me to do is get him to the bus station?" Michael asked as he looked back and forth at Gunslanga and Firebug.

"Not just that, because that'll be too easy

for you. It is now your job to take this Wade out," Firebug revealed as he leaned towards him.

The guy just looked over at Firebug and asked, "How do I know that you're not gonna leave me stinking?"

"You don't, but if you don't pull this off, that won't even be a question, now would it?" He replied with a sinister grin.

"I guess I really have no other choice."

"You don't seem too enthused about saving your own life," Gunslanga grilled.

★★★★★★★★★★★★★★

"How much do you have over there baby- girl?" Kruger was asking Deidra as they sat on her bed counting money.

"This is an even hundred," she replied as she placed rubber bands on every ten thousandth stack.

Kruger watched her and was amazed on how the money they were counting never seem to faze her. If you didn't know any better you would think that she counted this much money every day.

He knew that this was the first time that he'd seen this much money at one time, and inside he was more than excited. But with Deidra acting as if this was a few dollars in the cash register at her job, he knew he couldn't over- react.

"Well, I have like 72 stacks right here," he revealed.

"Well, let me get my book bag, I can put it in there," she replied as she raised from the bed and walked to her closet door.

"I'm gonna put 160 in the bag, you put ten up, and we'll find something to do with the two while we're in the Sea-Port."

"Baby, you know that I don't like you spending your money on me like that," is what she told him as she started shoving money in the bag.

"Don't you think it's about time for us to start shopping for the baby?" He implied knowing that if nothing else would put on smile on her face that implication would.

"Now you know that I'm down with that!" She excitedly responded.

"You know it's about time that we get our own crib," he stressed.

"I'm ready when you are," she replied.

"As soon as we can find a place, we can sit down with your daddy and my mama them and let it be known about our baby,"

"If that's all we've been waiting on, I'm on that first thing in the morning."

After a few moments of silence he asked, "Do your daddy have a girlfriend or something?"

"I don't know, but why you ask?"

"Cause it ain't no way that he had to work on a peaceful night in Augusta."

"You know that he be running behind Rev. Benny going from church to church every Sunday," she replied.

"Yeah, that's right," he stated with an aggravated expression before adding, "how can I forget that."

"There is nothing wrong with going to church, Deamon," she preached.

"I know that," was his response as if she had just insulted him, "I just hate being in church next to Sister Ford and Sister Gray, they always talking about people as if they were GOD themselves."

"They do be tripping, don't they," she agreed while trying control her laughter.

362

"But on the real though, I have no beef with church, it's the hypocrites that be off in there."

"You can't stop going to church because of how you see someone else is living, you have to go because of how you're trying to live," she attempted to explain with genuine concern.

"You right, but you have to understand that being around a lot of phony people makes my flesh crawl. When I was locked up all them cats that use to go to bible study and things like that, be the first ones to pull on the blunt when I playa lights one up. And to be honest with you, it really ain't no different out here. Most of the church members be there Sunday morning to repent for not wearing panties to the club that Saturday night."

"Deamon," she whined out in laughter, "you're sooo wrong!"

"Girl, I'm for real though," he stated, urging her to calm down, "I remember one time I was in church, I think we had a youth choir rehearsal or something. The deacon's wife called me to the back of the church, out of sight of everyone, and threw her dress over my head, and her old ass didn't even have panties on. After she did that I never said nothing else to her."

By this time Deidra was crying laughing. As soon as she regained her composure she told him, "I had no idea that you was this funny."

"I'm just trying to let you know that I have my own personal reasons why I ain't too fond of the church thing," is what he pointed out with a light chuckle of his own.

"Baby, if what happened to you, would have happened to me, I'd probably never go back either," she revealed as she eased up next to him and kissed him on the cheek before asking, "but why you ain't never tell nobody?"

"I did," he confessed, "I told Ron, and that fool just said that he hoped that she do him next."

Deidra just collapsed in his arms in laughter as she yelled out, "Deamon, stop it please, before you make me pee on myself!"

He then wrapped his arms around her causing her to calm down and they just sat there for a moment and gazed into each other's eyes. He knew at that moment that he had someone he had a genuine connection with. He knew that she was willing to do whatever for him.

"Let's go get something to eat," he finally suggested.

"Not until you kiss me," she demanded with a serious expression.

****

Michael sat on the bench by the pay phone at the Greyhound bus station. He'd just got off the phone with his former client. Gunslanga sat in the corner out of sight, while Firebug sat in the refreshment area waiting impatiently.

Gunslanga had briefed him on how to act when Big Wade came through the door, but from the look on Michael's face the only thing that was going through his mind was, run. In Michael's hand was his friend's Desert Eagle that contained only one bullet. The only reason he didn't just up and leave was the fact he knew that Gunslanga wouldn't hesitate to leave him full of holes right where he stood.

As he sat on the bench waiting on Big Wade, he thought about his friend, Stick-O, and how he caught his name.

It was their second hit and their client

allegedly had an altercation with the target. During the altercation, the target apparently told the client to go and fuck himself in front of a crowded restaurant, so the client wanted to send a message to everyone about how dangerous he really was.

Michael couldn't help but smile to himself after thinking of how the target looked after Stick-O cut off his dick and stuffed it in his ass. He was still smiling when Big Wade walked in the bus terminal.

With no hesitation he raised from his seat with the Desert Eagle aimed at his new target and squeezed the trigger. The bullet penetrated through Big Wade's nose, out of the back of his head and into the far wall.

When Firebug heard the shot, he ran toward the scene. Michael fled the scene as planned to his car they had a block away.

When Firebug and Gunslanga reached Big Wade's body, he was still alive. Gunslanga grabbed the bag from Big Wade's side that contained the money and just stood there and stared at Firebug for a moment.

"Why did it have to end like this, Wade?" Firebug asked as he stood over him with tears streaming down his cheeks, "Whatever it was, me and you should've been able to sit down and talk about it."

Gunslanga then stepped over Big Wade with one of Kruger's twins, to put Big Wade out of his misery, but Firebug snatched the gun from him and said, "This ain't your place youngblood."

Gunslanga looked at Firebug for a moment before turning and walking towards the same door Michael had just fled out of. By the time he made it to the door, he heard the gun shot. He didn't even have to turn around to see what happened.

****

"Say Burger," Red was saying as they sat on the porch along with Pimp and Black, "its something strange going on."

"What you mean?" Hamburger questioned.

"I mean here it is the eighth of the month and I haven't seen one narc car roll through all week," Red replied with a look of confusion.

"You know playboy, I was tripping off the

same shit," Black declared.

"I can't even call that one, but I can tell you that I ain't about to stress it either," Hamburger replied, "I ain't got but two ounces left, so as soon as I go through that I'm dipping for a minute."

"I can feel that," Red stressed, "because I'm gonna 50 pack these last five ounces I got before I cope this byrd."

"Dam nigga," Pimp stressed, "you working with byrd fare?"

"Dam right!" Red replied with aggression, "What, you think a nigga out here for his health?"

"Dam my nigga, you done came all the way up on a playa," Pimp inquired.

"I hate to be the one to burst your bubble baby-boy," Black interrupted, "but you're about the only one on the Summer working with less than a quarter byrd".

"Dam, I've been slipping like a muthafucka!" He stressed openly disgusted with himself.

"You need to get at that nigga Kruger, he been passing shit out for the low-low," Black informed.

"I'm gonna hollar at him just as soon as I finish this shit I got here."

"I think he out of town right now," Hamburger informed.

"Well I can wait until he gets back."

"What up with them cats Jimmy and Weasel?" Red asked with a devilish grin.

Kruger had already told the fellas about Weasel's phone call, so Red just wanted to see what Pimp had to say.

"Man, that nigga Weasel wanted to jack the prices on a playa," he replied before adding, "you don't expect that from your own flesh and blood."

"Sweet prices don't last for a lifetime," Hamburger stated, "I wouldn't care if it was your mama with the dope."

Pimp nodded his head in agreement as if everything was making since now.

"Dam that, where the hell is Butler?" Black asked.

"He in the back somewhere frying his brain," Red replied.

"Let him be," Black stated, "he done put

in some major work this week."

"Well somebody need to check on him cause I just broke him off a few grams, so he might have fried himself to death back there," Hamburger implied causing everyone to burst out laughing.

-KRUGER-

Man I can't even begin to understand what the hell went on with Firebug and Big Wade. Slanga's ass is over at Teresa's old apartment probably more boggled than I am, and he say he heard and saw everything first hand.

Here I am in this hotel room trying to contemplate what's really good. I sent Deidra shopping with Amanda and the twins so I can marinate on this bullshit. I could've stayed at Teresa's apartment with Slanga so we can discuss this a little more, but I felt that I would've been disrespecting Deidra and Teresa, besides I need some time to clear my mind.

Despite everything else that's on my mind, I still can't phantom what the hell Big Wade was thinking about? I mean how could he cross his own people like that? To me this is some real live television shit!

It's like we're all in a movie and everybody has their own script that no-one but that person can read. If it is like that, I'm improvising mine. I mean if GOD has actually gave me a scene like that in my script than I guess I'll be dying in a car accident or something, cause I ain't violating the codes of the streets.

Man, I ain't so shallow minded to lay her and think that life is that sweet and there won't be no obstacles I have to go through or whatever. But I also ain't so lame to think that I can actually be successful by snaking my own either. To keep it genuine with a playa is far better than keeping it 100, and that's the business right there. I'll take a dude who genuine with whatever, before I take a nigga who claim he 100. Because when it all boils down, I don't know what the cat, who says he 100, extremes are. A genuine cat is non-hypocritical, he can't attempt to be something that he's not, if he does, you know he ain't genuine.

Me and Slanga suppose to meet up and hollar at Firebug later to make sure he still sane, cause Slanga say that he ain't been taking this thing to well. Hell, that shit probably would have me fucked up too.

STUCK

You would think that if you and your peoples have differences, you would be able to sit down and discuss it cause that's your peoples, but most of these friendships are just that, friendships. I mean, there is no brotherly love, well at least not on both ends. I mean, we blind to that genuine brotherly love for each other, because most of us have the wrong motives.

To me, there is nothing in this world that can replace the genuine love you possess for you peoples. You can have all the money in the world, but you could never be totally happy without your closest people by your side. Money don't make a person, to me it only brings forth the true reality of who that person really is.

I know that the old man feels kind of crazy about pulling that trigger himself, but in a situation like that, he really had no choice. They say in this game, anything goes, and from that situation, I kind of see where that saying comes from. That's like me crossing Slanga, when he's the main reason I'm in the position I'm in. That's preposterous!

I guess in time we all realize who's truly down with us and who ain't. Like Big Jay told me, "Most cats claim friends for what you are, not who you are!"

****

"WHETHER YOU WIN OR LOSE IN LIFE ITS DO OR DIE, BUT SOMETIMES YOU LOSE THE WILL TO WIN AND WONDER WHY!" Is what Scarface was humming through the speakers of Amanda's Altima as Kruger and Gunslanga was riding to meet Firebug at *Longhorn's*.

"Thank GOD for cats like Scarface on that music tip," Kruger was saying.

"Yeah, I can feel that," Gunslanga agreed, "it's like he keeps a song for times like this."

"It ain't just him," Kruger retorted, "its music period! If it wasn't for music it would be a lot of insane people walking around."

"Yeah, even I've calmed down a lot since I smooth up my music," Gunslanga revealed.

"Don't tell me that you were around here booty shaking?" Kruger stressed with a light chuckle.

"Hell na'll!" He retorted, "Nigga, you know what I'm talking about."

"Playboy, you know I had to sneak that one in. you left it too open. But yeah, I know where you're coming from. But, that just goes to show you how another muthafuckas can perceive the wrong thing."

"Yeah," Gunslanga agreed, "we definitely have to watch what we say around certain cats. Haters are always trying to find flaws in another muthafucka."

"Point seen!" Kruger stressed, "If cats would tend to their own as much as they try to tend to the next man's, they'll be on top in no time."

"Yeah, that's definitely a point seen. You know, another way we can look at it is, while they got their mind on us, we can be raking up all the cheese."

"True," Kruger agreed with a sly grin.

"So, let them fools continue to do what they do, just as long as neither one of us don't get caught in that mind frame, we good," he replied as he pulled in the parking-lot next to Firebug's Seville.

"Playboy, I don't think that we have to worry about that with us," he replied as he hopped out of the passenger side.

"Say," Gunslanga implied, "you ain't never told me the outcome on ole boy with the

Chevy."

"You know that's all good," Kruger replied with a sly grin as he opened the door for his comrade, "money is the root of all evil, remember?"

Gunslanga paused at the door with a smirk of his own before saying, "I thought pussy was the root of all evil?"

"Na'll playboy," he replied while patting him on the back, "you must ain't heard Bun B, pussy is the root of all drama."

After they found their way to the table where Firebug was waiting patiently, they embraced the old man.

"How you doing pop?" Kruger asked.

"I'm holding up," he replied with a light smile, "I'm just focused on getting this money right now. Ya'll know how we had to handle situations when we was locked up?"

They both nodded their head.

"Same thing, just a different atmosphere. Like your boy 2-Pac said, you gotta hold your head!"

"Dam pop," Kruger stressed with a smile of approval, "you surprised me with that one."

"You shouldn't be," he replied with a smile of his own, "they had me trapped in a two man cell with this youngun for eighteen months, so you know I'm all up on that."

Kruger and Gunslanga just looked over at each other and burst out laughing.

"What the hell are ya'll laughing at?" Firebug questioned.

"It ain't nothing really," Gunslanga replied, "it's just on our way over here we were just talking about how music soothes the soul."

"That's overstood," Firebug replied before asking, "but what's the deal with ya'll on this business tip?"

"Well you know that I done been here the whole time, but I think Kruger done came up with 160 stacks," Gunslanga revealed.

"Dam youngblood!" Firebug excitedly responded, "Now if you're working with that much, I can't help but give you these last 16, and all I want is 15 a piece for the extra six."

"Now that's right on time," Kruger replied with a broad smile.

"Now, that's the best I can do," Firebug confessed, "but don't look for it to be like that all the time. It's just that I'm trying to make a move and I already know I'm a need that bread."

"Say no more!" Kruger excitedly responded, "What's understood doesn't need to be talked about!"

STUCK